The Poppy Killings

By Paul F Smith

Prologue

In days of old before computers, mobile phones, radio, body cams and even DNA, the police when investigating crimes had a card index in each police station in an office called the collators. The collator would collate crimes and criminals, all people who came to the attention of the police. Prior to 1968 every city and town had its own police force called a constabulary and they would have a senior officer in charge sometimes called a Chief Constable.

In 1968 the Metropolitan Police in London started what we now know as a department called SOCO (Scenes of Crime Officers). Before then every investigating officer of a crime would search for fingerprints, scraps of clothing, blood and footprints, what we now call forensic evidence. Sometimes the constabulary would have a designated fingerprint officer, the forerunner of SOCO. When a person was arrested and taken to the police station they might have their fingerprints taken and that would be two sets. One set would be kept at the police station (after 1968 at a central building for that county) the other set would be sent to Scotland Yard. In those olden days it was all about paper.

The collator would have a massive card index of all the people who had come to the attention of the police in that Constabulary. He would also have a wanted board of persons who had failed to appear on police or the court bail. In those days he was the nerve centre if a constable or detective needed information on someone. If the person was CRO (had a Criminal Record Office number) then Scotland Yard could be contacted to find out what that person had been arrested for previously.

This entirely fictitious story is set in Doncaster in 1963 and at that time they had Detective Officers not Detective Constables, why? I have no idea. Perhaps it was a quirk of their Chief Constable because the initials DO were the first two letters of Doncaster.

Maungy Miller

It was Saturday 3rd August 1963. Steve Bowers walked to the library and tried the door handle, it was locked. He looked at his wristwatch, 10am. The library should be open by now. Maungy Miller the librarian was renowned for two things, his miserable face and his timekeeping.

It was Steve's day off and yesterday his wife Julie had announced that she was pregnant with their first child. Steve was here to find a book on the mysteries of pregnancy and child birth. He was a detective officer at Doncaster Police Station.

He tried the door again. Nothing, so he went round the back to the fire door. He knew that Miller sometimes left the door ajar to let some air in. Sure enough it was open. He went in past the small kitchen and into the library proper, he could see Miller's jacket hanging up in his office. He went past a stair that led to a conference room. He arrived at the desk that Miller normally sat at.

"Mr Miller are you there?" he shouted up the stairs, nothing. He went up to the front door and could see the keys in the lock, ready to open up. Today being a Saturday, the assistant wouldn't be there because on a Saturday the library would shut at 2pm. Steve thought perhaps he is in the gents. He opened the door went down the steps and then through the door to the gents toilets. Inside he was faced with 3 sinks, 3 urinals on the left and 3 cubicles on the right. The middle one was almost closed. Very gingerly Steve pushed open the door. What he saw stopped him in his tracks, he was gobsmacked.

Sitting on the toilet with his trousers down was a very dead looking Mr Miller. He was leaning into the left hand partition and there was something jammed in his throat, with a small trickle of blood down the collar of his shirt. Very carefully Steve felt for a pulse. Nothing. Instinctively he looked at his watch, ten minutes past ten. He left the gents raced up the stairs to the small office and then rang the police station, he said to Daisy the telephonist "CID sergeants". She put him through.

Detective Sergeant Frank Dipper answered the telephone.

"Sarge, its Steve. I'm at the library and Miller is in the gents, dead as a doornail with something jammed in his throat."

"Okay Steve," Frank said calmly. "Do not touch anything, lock the front door and open the rear door."

"The front is locked anyway and the back is open."

"Okay. Stay by that door and don't let anyone in. I'm on my way."

15 minutes later Frank arrived with local bobbys, PCs Jack Bradley and Dennis Parkin.

Frank said "Dennis, man this door, find some paper, you know the drill, it's now twenty-five minutes past ten. Log that. Steve, lead the way."

Steve, Frank and Jack went down the stairs into the toilets. "Hands in pockets chaps."

Frank looked at Miller. "Very undignified, looks a bit like a spade blade in his throat, Doctor Wells is on his way as should be Ink and Blot." These were the nicknames for the two designated fingerprint officers Rod Elway and John Benson. Several minutes later in walked the doctor.

"Well, well poor old Leonard what a way to go." Said Doctor Wells, the pathologist who would do the post mortem. "Definitely dead. Looking at the tiny amount of blood I would say he has been strangled somewhere else and then dumped in here." Just then Ink and Blot appeared.

Doctor Wells said "I will get out of your way. Try to leave that metal in his throat, my boys from the morgue should be here in about 25 minutes, they are scraping someone up from the A1." He went upstairs with Frank, Steve and Jack. Doctor Wells had a look around and then left.

Frank said to Steve "Seeing as you were the first on the scene you will be the exhibits officer so that metal blade will be SB/1. Here are some exhibit bags. Get Miller's jacket, wallet, anything valuable and bag it up. Jack, as the local bobby, what time does Miller normally get here?

Jack said "Monday to Saturday he gets here at 7.30am come rain or shine with the cleaner Doris Jenkins, she leaves always at 8.30am. She is very thorough. Can't you smell the polish and the disinfectant in the toilet? Doris lives with him but believe me it is very platonic. Weekdays the library is open 9am to 6pm but he normally buggers off about 4 leaving the assistant, today he would have closed up at 1pm."

Frank said "So the killer watches the cleaner leave and then comes in the back and does him between then and 10am when Steve gets here."

Just then Ink and Blot came back upstairs. Ink said "Not a lot down there no prints, we have taken photographs so he is ready for the mortuary boys. We had a look at the fire door when we came in and it is very clean so either the killer was wearing gloves or gave the handle a good wipe." They then had a good look around the desk and Ink said "Clean as a baby's bottom. Not a single print." They then left.

Frank said "Steve, you stay here until the mortuary team arrive and then lock up, can you put a notice on the front door, library closed until further notice. Jack and Dennis do a bit of house to house, the church at the back and then I will see you back at the nick. I'll now go and tell the Chief what has happened and find out who the SIO (Senior Investigating Officer) is going to be. See you all later." He picked up the bagged items and returned to the police station.

The Chief

Frank went down to the collator's office. Reginald Prestleigh, a collator famous for his magnificent quiff and Elvis impressions, had set up the incident room next to his office, complete with boards that would hold all the information relating to the murder.

Reg said "So who do you think we will get as an SIO, probably a Met Superintendent."

Frank said "I'm going to see the Chief now and we shall soon know."

20 minutes later Frank returned to the collators. In the incident room was a large locker that would be used to put in the various exhibits. Frank put Miller's possessions in until they could be given to his housekeeper. Reg rattled a tin at Frank "the tea fund is now up and running, please donate."

Frank said "I'm feeling generous so here is ten shillings and mine is a mug of tea no sugar."

Reg put the kettle on and said "So did the Chief say who our boss will be?"

"No. He is coming down later when we are all gathered together." Steve came in and wrote out an exhibit label ready for the metal blade shoved in Miller's throat. He made himself a mug of coffee. 30 minutes later in walked Jack and Dennis.

Jack said to Frank "We went to the shops which as you know are about 50 yards from the library, nothing to talk about there but at the church I saw Father Dominic. On the Thursday before a man went into the church and asked Dom what time the library opened today. Dom told him the opening time and he left. The description is male 40 to 45 years 6 foot or so, well built, clean shaven, bit of a posh accent wearing black mechanics overalls, black boots and a cap comforter."

"What is a cap comforter?" Steve asked.

Frank said "Oh come on Steve you did National Service, it's a military scarf that can be turned into a cap."

Jack said "Dom felt that he had a bit of a military bearing."

Frank said "Did he have a vehicle perhaps?"

"No, I'll do a statement now and will get one from Dom" Jack said.

Just then the Chief walked in, everyone stood up. George Dawson was always called the Chief and he had never been seen on duty in anything other than his immaculate uniform. His medal ribbons showed that he had served in the First World War, now 65 years of age he was very close to retirement.

"Gentlemen please sit down and Reg a black tea no sugar." He took the mug and sat down. "I have made several telephone calls and normally we would have a Metropolitan Police Superintendent as the SIO. The Commissioner has said they are tucked up with several murders in the Home Counties so I have decided that we shall have one of our own. Detective Chief Inspector Ralph Renton is up and coming, he is currently helping out York City Police but will be here on Monday, so Frank if you will run the ship until he arrives. I trust you will treat him gently and we will come to a speedy conclusion in arresting Leonard Miller's killer. I will leave you to talk tactics and take this fine mug of tea with me."

He stood up as did everyone else.

Once he had gone Jack said "That's the last we will see of that mug."

Just then in walked Austin Bradley, Jack's dad. Austin was a retired police sergeant. He had joined Doncaster police after the First World War with George Dawson. Later promoted to sergeant he had been responsible for the bobbys who policed the mining villages between Doncaster and Barnsley.

"I bring gifts," he said. He opened a cake tin to reveal 8 buttered fruit scones compliments of the wife. "So what's been happening today?" Frank explained about Miller.

Austin said "Poor old Maungy not a pleasant way to die and sat on the pot. So the last person to see him die would have been dear old Doris the cleaner, you had better cop a statement then lad," he said to Jack.

"She goes to the church behind the library, I will see her tomorrow and fix up a time. I have telephoned the bobby in Tickhill to break the news."

"More to the point does anyone know this Ralph Renton?" Steve said.

Austin said "I remember him joining, ex Intelligence Corps in the second war. Clever lad, grammar school then constable to Detective Chief Inspector in 15 years. Not bad."

DI Johnny Martin walked in "A bit of a golden balls type I think." Johnny was a local lad and well liked by all, he was a good thief taker.

Frank went through it all again and just as he finished in walked Dr. Wells.

"Hello chaps how is it going? I thought I would pop in and give you a basic rundown on Leonard's death. Full report will be ready on Monday. He was sitting down when he was strangled. He had been tied to his chair and gagged. Leonard wasn't that big and about 10 stone wringing wet but his assailant was powerful. After conveying him to the porcelain he then jammed this in his throat. He died somewhere between 8am to 9am, that's about the best I can do."

Austin looked at the blade "This is the sharp end of a First World War entrenching tool, issued to every Private for digging holes, latrines and very handy in close combat when you were low on ammo."

Frank said "So why use the spade after he died? A bit theatrical."

Dr. Wells said "I am no psychologist but perhaps when he gagged and tied Leonard to the chair perhaps he told him what he was going to do to him after he strangled him, a sort of power over your victim thing."

Steve said "Did you know Mr. Miller well?"

"Oh yes. I have a part share in a racehorse and would often see him at the races. He was sarcastic sober and downright obnoxious when drunk. Anyway, must dash. Will give you the full SP on Monday say 4ish." He then left.

Frank said "Make up your pocket books for today and I will see you all tomorrow at 10am after morning prayers."

Renton

Frank arrived at 8.30am, went down to the collators and made himself a nice strong mug of tea.

On a Sunday the Chief liked to attend church at 10am, before that he would meet the senior heads of departments at 9am to discuss anything that had arisen in the previous 24 hours or so, this meeting was known as 'morning prayers.' Frank finished his tea and went upstairs leaving Reg typing up his cards. Each card would have a criminal's name, current address and previous conviction so if he had been arrested or charged or attended court, the result would be typed onto the card. Also, there would be any suspicious sightings of him and associates. The cards were joined by sticky tape, concertina fashion.

Steve arrived just before 10am and made himself a coffee and then put 5 shillings in the kitty. In came Austin, followed by Ink. Frank came in next with Johnny Martin.

Ink said to Frank "Here is a statement basically saying that the library was devoid of any prints apart from a couple on a desk drawer which must be Miller's. I'll go to the mortuary tomorrow and get his prints for elimination purposes. Hopefully we will have some photographs tomorrow of Miller."

Ink left and Reg said to Frank "Anything from prayers? I see there was some criminal damage and Eric Cooper was arrested yet again for drunk pestering the staff at the railway station."

Austin said "Well, well, our SIO is here." Everyone stood up except Austin who saluted.

Ralph Renton, now the Senior Investigating Officer, walked in, greeted his new colleagues and said "Reg, here is a one pound note for the kitty I'm sure you have. Mine is a strong black coffee no sugar, thank you."

He looked at Austin and said "Well I know this old chap." He shook Austin's hand "Just here as a consultant I presume. I know Johnny and you Frank we have met before."

"Yes," Frank said "In the war. I recall you speak French and helped me to get a cup of tea not far from Paris."

"And this young feller is?"

Steve said "DO Steve Bowers sir."

Renton sat down with the others and said "I suppose I should tell you a bit about myself, ignore anything that Austin has said. I was born in Harrogate. Both my parents were killed in a car crash when I was 3 and I was adopted by my dad's cousin. My mum, I never used the word step-mum, my mum was a French Jew and she taught me French and a bit of Hebrew. I also learnt to speak German and a bit of Spanish. I enlisted in the Intelligence Corps and near the end of the war met Frank Dipper. 1945 I joined Doncaster Police and later went to York City Police. So that is me. Tell me about Leonard Miller and what you have so far."

Frank then told him about the murder and showed him the blade.

"I see. SB/1. I take it that is you Steve?"

"Yes sir, I am now the exhibits officer for the murder."

"Very good and what about this cleaner?"

Austin said "My lad Jack has gone to the church to see her and make an appointment to take a statement. She was the last one to see Miller alive."

Renton said "Austin, you probably knew Miller better than anyone here. Can you give us an idea about him?"

"I reckon Miller was about 70 or thereabouts. Why he carried on working after retiring as an Inspector I'm not sure but maybe it was to keep a certain type of lifestyle. He was single, never married and rumour was he was a bit of a Jessie. According to my pals in the Legion he had an easy war, that's the first one, working in the stores at Etaples. After that lot he joined the Met. He got here in 1945. No doubt his chums in the Lodge got him the senior librarian job. He lived with his mum in Tickhill. Doris was the cleaner at the library and she became his mum's carer and companion. She moved in the house when mum died and became Miller's housekeeper. Doris and my Hilda meet once a week and she did say it is a very platonic relationship."

"Well, thank you for that Austin, very comprehensive as always. There is not a lot I can do at the moment. The Chief is going to welcome me officially tomorrow so I will see you all then."

Frank said "Where are you staying?"

"Fortunately with my Aunt Alice Maud in Warmsworth, 72 years old, sharp as a tack but a great cook, just a bit religious."

Jack came in, Austin introduced him to Renton.

Jack said "I have Doris in the front office, can I take the car, give her a lift home and take the statement at the same time?"

Renton said "Perfect, why not."

Frank gave him the car keys and Jack left.

Renton said to Frank and Steve "Sort out any paperwork on your desks. Reg, can you start a timeline on Miller from what Austin has said and a description of the killer that Father Dominic gave us and I will see you all tomorrow."

Doris Jenkins

Jack took Doris home to the detached house in Tickhill. It was Victorian with an imposing front door with two bay windows either side. On the first floor were 3 large windows.

They went inside and Doris led the way into the kitchen. "I will make a pot of tea, I am sure you must be gasping. I am." She produced 2 cups and saucers and a couple of slices of homemade lemon cake. Having poured the tea she said "I am now ready."

Jack said "What can you tell me about Miller and his life?"

She opened a cupboard and pulled out a polished wooden box. "He was going to write his memoirs but this is a far as he got." She handed Jack a piece of paper.

He read "I was born on 14th October 1895 in Putney in London. My father John was a gentlemen's tailor, my mother was a housewife and kept the home. I was sent to a private school when I was six, it was tough and I hated it but I did get a very good education. I finished at 16 and trained to be an accountant but in 1913 I joined the Metropolitan Police employed in their accountancy department. 1914 arrived and I enlisted. Because of my background in accountancy, I was put into the Royal Engineers in charge of the stores, the Postal Section and ordnance at a large base at Etaples in France."

Jack said "So what happened after that?"

"He made a few friends and with them he joined the Metropolitan Police. Being smaller than most of them he, again, was used in an office job, something to do with their records department. He said because it was the biggest force in the country he was kept very busy. He must have been very good because by 1935 he was an Inspector. His father was killed in the Blitz so his mother moved in with him. They sold her house and made quite bit of money. He retired in 1945 and moved here to this house. His friends got him the job in the library. I started there in 1950. He asked me to help out with his mum which I did. When she died he asked me to stay on as his housekeeper. I had my own bedroom and the lounge and his territory was the study."

Jack said "Do you have anything from his military career?"

From the box she produced Miller's medals and a photograph which she gave to Jack. The photograph showed 4 men sitting at a table covered in plates of food and some bottles of wine. To one side was a young orderly holding a tray of glasses. On the back the caption read "Etaples Christmas 1916 and the gang."

Jack said "Which one is Mr. Miller?"

She said "He was taking the photograph. The camera is in his study." She pulled out an envelope "This came 3 weeks ago."

It was a letter, no address, no stamp with just 'Mr. L Miller' written on it. He opened the envelope and took out a sheet of paper, written on it was "TUG, SPIDER, MAC, TOMMO, DUSTY." Spider and Mac had a line drawn through the name. Inside the envelope was a British Legion poppy with the word 'Etaples' written on it.

Jack said "Quality paper. What did Mr. Miller think about this?"

"He just thought it was some sort of a joke."

"I will take the statement now about you being the last person to see Mr. Miller alive."

Jack said "So you both get to the library at 7.30am every day except Sunday and you leave by 8.30am leaving the fire door just slightly open."

"Yes. That is right."

Jack wrote the statement, she read it through and then signed it and Jack endorsed it.

Jack said "Do you have any other photographs from the war and from when he was a policeman?"

"Yes, follow me."

She led him to the study, unlocked the door and they went in. Jack just stood there gobsmacked. One wall on the left was covered in photographs showing army life in the war, the other wall had nearly as many of policemen. Under the window was his desk with a scrapbook of newspaper cuttings, a bottle of brandy and one of whisky and a glass. They walked back out into the hall and she locked the door.

Jack said "I think I need to bring the boss to have a look at this, let's say tomorrow about 1pm, also can I take the box? I will give you a receipt for it and it will be returned at the end of the investigation."

Jack returned to the station and showed the others the photograph from the box.

Austin said "I knew it he had a bloody easy war."

Reg said "I'll put it in the locker until tomorrow and let our SIO look at it."

Introductions

Frank arrived at the police station at 8.30am, it was Monday 5th August. He looked in his tray. There was a note from Margery, the Chief's secretary, saying he would bring the new SIO to the incident room at 10.30 after morning prayers. He went down to the collators and told Reg about the Chief's message and said "Contact the troops and have them all here for 10am sharp, I am still clearing the mess that is my desk, see you later."

At 10am Frank arrived back in the collators and gradually the others came in. Father and son, Austin and Jack were first, followed by Dennis and his old pal Ted Maynard. Steve Bowers arrived with Johnny Martin and finally in came DO David Tinsley and WDO Tina Shaw, both freshly assigned to the investigation. Frank said "Make yourselves a drink and all be in the incident room ready for the Chief".

10.30am. In walked the Chief with Renton. Everyone stood up and the Chief motioned them to sit down and said "I would like to introduce you all to Detective Chief Inspector Ralph Renton, he is a Yorkshire lad and so I think he will do well with you all. I won't embarrass him asking for a speech and all that twaddle. I will leave you to get to know each other and then get on with catching Leonard Miller's killer."

The Chief then left, everyone stood up and then relaxed. Renton said "Let's all have a drink and then talk business."

Frank then introduced everyone to Renton.

Renton said "In the incident room I would like the chairs in a semi circle and the table in the middle. We will brief and debrief in there. That will allow Reg to get on with his work. I am told that the exhibits will be locked in the locker in the corner. Frank can you give us all the details so far from Steve finding the body and show the exhibit you have."

Frank ran through what had taken place right up to Jack taking Mrs Jenkins statement, he put the blade down on the table for David and Tina to have a look at it. He pointed out the 2 initials on the back of the blade. W.M. He then said "Over to you Jack."

Jack then explained what Mrs. Jenkins had said about Miller and he produced the letter, with the poppy and the note with the nicknames on it.

Renton said "Now, for our younger members these nicknames traditionally go with surnames so 'Dusty' Miller, 'Spider' Webb and 'Tug' Wilson, however Mac must be short for MacDonald or something similar and Tommo must be short for Thomas, either a first name or a surname. Also, this photograph is possibly those people, apparently the photographer was always Miller. These exhibits for the time being will be JB/1 and JB/2. Here we have an address book belonging to Miller. I would like David and Tina to make out a list of everyone on it and then contact by telephone all on it or visit all those in the Doncaster area. Steve and Dennis, grab Peter Johns from the next office, he knows a thing or two about fingerprints and go out and about in Doncaster with the description of cap comforter man. I am told that Doctor Wells will be coming in at 5pm so everyone back here by 4.30pm at the latest."

He turned to Jack "12.30 you can drive Frank and me to Tickhill and we will have a look at this study, so everyone get to it but first I would like to go to the library."

15 minutes later they were in the library. Jack showed Renton the toilets. Renton then said "Frank if you can sit at the desk and I will be the killer. Tell me if you hear any sounds as I come in through the fire door." Renton opened the fire door, went outside almost closing the door and then very quietly opened it and crept up to Frank and put his hands on Frank's shoulders.

Renton said "So did you hear anything at all Frank?"

"Not a thing."

"Presumably the killer shut the fire door after killing Miller." said Renton "Then down to the toilets and then out, without leaving a single fingerprint. Very efficient. Looking at the crossings out of the nicknames I would hazard a guess he has killed 2 of this merry band already. Righto let us go and see the cleaner. Let the council know they can re-open the library."

The Study

As they left the library Renton said "Any chance of a cuppa somewhere on the way?"

Jack drove to Dick's Diner and once inside Renton ordered 3 bacon rolls, a coffee and 2 mugs of tea for Frank and Jack. "Is this one of your tea spots?" Renton said to Jack.

"Yes," Jack said "Dick supplies food for prisoners when our canteen is shut. His meals are very nice. Open 6.30am and closes 4pm. Breakfast to 11am then 3 mains, 3 puddings. Deals for pensioners in the winter, soup and a sandwich."

"I might come here then for my lunch."

25 minutes later they arrived at the house in Tickhill. Jack knocked on the door and introduced Renton and Frank to Mrs. Jenkins.

She said "I remember Frank. Cheeky little sod as I remember. Come into the kitchen and I will make a cuppa. She produced a cake tin and cut a slice for each of them.

They sat down and enjoyed their cake and then Renton said "I am told that Leonard never married?"

"No, he preferred the company of men. He stayed in touch with his pals he had met in the war and in the police. They would meet up at the races here and in York and once a year all go to Ascot and stay in a posh hotel. I think they were all Freemasons you know."

Having finished his drink and cake, Renton said "Can we look in the study?"

She led them to the study, unlocked the door and gave the keys to Jack. They walked in and on seeing the walls of pictures Renton said "My God

Jack you were not wrong." He looked around and said to Frank "You look at the police photos and I will look at the war ones and select say 5 that show a different range of people other than the 4 we saw in the first photo."

While they were doing that Jack sat at the desk and went through its drawers. Stationery, old newspaper cuttings, cigars. In the bottom draw was a cigar box tied up with string. He undid the string and opened the box. It had some more photographs inside. The first one showed several men being inspected by an officer outside a cafe, in the distance Jack could see the Eiffel Tower. The second one showed 4 men naked lying on couches while a scantily clad waitress was serving them drinks. The caption on the back said "Champagne time Paris Christmas 1918." Jack said "You had better look at this boss."

Renton and Frank looked at the photograph. Frank said "Brothel. You don't get waitresses dressing like that in a regular restaurant."

The third photograph showed several men in shorts paddling in the sea, with a young orderly holding several towels and not looking very happy. The caption on the back said "Le Touquet 1917 with Steady Eddy always ready."

The fourth photograph showed 4 men in uniform holding glasses and the young orderly holding a champagne bottle, again not looking very happy. The caption on the back was "It will be all over by Christmas 1915."

Frank said "The tallest one is an officer, you can see his Sam Browne belt."

Jack had found a cardboard box and they put the framed photographs from the walls and the cigar box of photographs in it. When they had left the study Jack locked it up and gave the key to Mrs. Jenkins.

Renton said to her "We are taking some of the photographs with us. I will give you a receipt and they will be returned at the end of the investigation. What will happen to you now that Leonard has died?"

She said "He has left me the house in his will and quite a bit of money so I am very comfortable. I will give some money to the church in his memory."

Renton said "Thank you for the tea and the cake. I will keep you informed."

With that they returned to the station.

Debrief

They arrived back at the station and spread the framed photographs out on the table in the briefing room. Renton gave the cigar box to Reg and said "Have a look at its contents and then lock it up in your desk. That is not for public consumption until I have shown the Chief."

Reg looked at the photographs and said "Don't show Austin, he will lose it for sure."

By 4.30pm everyone had arrived and made a drink, Reg rattled the tin at David and Tina, who donated ten shillings each.

Renton asked them to look at the various framed photographs on the table."As you can see they revolve around 6 people, the young orderly who we know is called Eddy. Now the nicknames we have seen must be the four main people in the photographs. Dusty we know is Miller who took all these photographs. Now Spider and Mac have a line drawn through them so is this an indication that they are already dead. David and Tina, how did you get on with Miller's address book."

Tina said "The only name corresponding to the 5 names in the letter was a Mary Thomas who died in 1960 in London, her daughter said that she had worked for the Mets in an office at Scotland Yard. No Wilsons or Webbs or Scottish names beginning with Mac. Out of the 15 names 12 are now dead. 2 are in old people's homes in Lincoln and the other one, who is 83, lives in Armthorpe and her daughter said she had been a secretary in the British Legion in York."

"Steve and Dennis, did you get anything?"

"We shared the description around shops and garages in Doncaster just as you said, but got nothing. It seems most mechanics are under 6 foot and covered in oil or petrol. We had a look around the church and graveyard and nobody there wanted to talk."

There was a ripple of laughter. Even Renton smiled.

Renton said "So we concentrate on Miller. Birth to death. Steve contact the Mets' personnel department and find out if he worked in just one place or moved around. They can send us his record I am sure. Ask if anyone remembers him and who did he mix with. David, Ministry of Defence, where would we get the list of people who served in Etaples in the Postal Section at the same time Miller? Peter and Tina, the racecourse, do they have any records or photographs of him? Anything really."

Just as Renton finished, in came Dr. Wells "Hope I'm not too early chaps and lady." Tina blushed.

Frank introduced him to Renton.

Dr. Wells said "Leonard Miller was punched in the face possibly to stun him, tied to a chair very tightly including his legs so he could not stand up and gagged. Then from behind the killer, who I would say about 6 foot, exerted pressure on Miller as he strangled him. Miller tried to resist because he had chafing on his legs as he pushed against the chair trying to move forward but to no avail. Any question's so far?"

Steve said "Why tie him up and not just strangle him?"

"Yes, very good young man. Perhaps the killer wanted to say something to him. With that blade shoved in his throat and being placed on the pot with his trousers down, I would surmise that is something only known to Miller and his killer. Some form of humiliation. Power over your victim."

Steve said "How long would it take from punching Mr Miller to the killer leaving by the back door?"

"Yes, good question. I would say no more than 30 minutes.

"Why wasn't there more blood with that blade in his throat?"

"Once the killer had strangled him his heart would stop beating and then the blood would start to clot but also the blade missed his main artery. Also, the killer was very tidy, taking the rope and gag with him. To me that would suggest that he has killed before and I am told there wasn't a single fingerprint. Any more questions?"

Silence.

"I shall be off." He nodded to Renton who walked him to the door.

Out of earshot of the others the Doctor said "I like that young man he asked all the right questions."

After seeing the doctor out, Renton said to Frank "Very brisk our doctor?"

Frank said "Yes he was in the RAMC. Landed on D-Day with Jack and Ted and went all the way to the Fatherland."

Renton said "You all know what you are doing. I will be in the Red Lion at 6pm and my wallet will be open for business for exactly 10 minutes. Jack and Dennis, I will see you tomorrow for your tasks."

Hit and Run

The next morning Renton was in the incident room looking at the photographs when Jack came in.

Jack said "I thought I would have an early breakfast in the Diner and gave him the description of cap comforter man. Dick said that on Thursday last week a man fitting that description came in and asked where the library was. Dick told him this was about 12 noon. The man had something to eat, steak pie and chips and no gravy. Had to be a southerner, I mean no gravy that's a hanging offence round here. The man then drove off in a black Commer van. I will go back later and take a statement."

Just then Dennis walked in and said "You have a special mission for Jack and me boss?"

Before he could reply in walked Frank with Austin, "I found this old boy loitering outside." Austin punched him on the arm "Anytime son, you and me?"

Renton said "I would put my money on Austin, you know how tricky those Marines were. Now Dennis and Jack I want you to contact all the main collators in offices across the 3 Ridings, so Bradford, Sheffield, York, Harrogate. Reg will give you the Almanac. All deaths of retired police officers either by accident or otherwise, maybe someone is targeting them like they did Miller. At some stage Jack get that statement from the Diner. I will leave you to it and see you at debrief." He then said to Austin "Tell me about Etaples?"

Austin said "Awful place, a massive camp where the railway went straight into the hospitals. The wounded would come back from the front, would be patched up, retrained and sent back to the trenches. The retraining was carried out by instructors who had never been at the front. There was a small scale mutiny which was hushed up because they thought it might spread to the trenches. No doubt one day the truth will come out. Etaples is now one big cemetery."

Renton then showed him the framed photographs and said to Reg "Can you pass me the cigar box?" He then handed it to Austin. "Have a look at these."

Austin sat down and went through the photographs. He handed them back to Renton and said "I said they were a bunch of skivers and those photographs show you what a bunch of degenerates they were."

It was 2pm and Renton had just arrived back at his desk from lunch when his telephone rang. He answered it to find it was a colleague from York, DI Bill Reynolds.

"Hello Ralph how are you. Our collator received a telephone call from one of your lads asking if we had any deaths of a retired police officer. He contacted me because we have an ongoing case that started as a heart attack as a result of a hit and run here in York in February. You were away at the time in London on that attempted murder trial at the Old Bailey. The man who died was a George MacCrae. Why don't you come over tomorrow and I will give you all the details."

"Great idea, I will see you tomorrow say about 11am."

Renton went down to the incident room and said to Dennis "We have had a hit in York, retired copper died in a hit and run accident in February this year so that is our man MAC and that is why he has a line through his name, so Spider Webb could also be dead."

Debrief arrived as did everyone else, they all made themselves a drink then Renton said "Steve, what of the personnel department of the Mets?"

Steve said "He only worked in one place which was Scotland Yard. By the time he made inspector he was in charge of all the records of the people who worked in the police. They found someone who remembered him.

She said he wasn't liked due to being sarcastic and arrogant and they were glad to see the back of him."

"David, what about the military?"

"Ministry of Defence said that they are not allowed to divulge anything about the military before 1939.They suggested the National Archives who I rang and they will send us a form for us to fill in on what we know about him. However I did say that we know he only served at Etaples. They said that is all they would have as well."

"Wonderful, Peter and Tina?"

Peter said "We talked to a couple of stewards at the racecourse and they said to talk to some chap who used to come in and take photographs of the punters which they could then buy, but they couldn't remember which one it was in Doncaster."

"Righto, I have some news. A retired copper was the victim of a hit and run in York in February this year. He had a heart attack at the scene and apparently the vehicle was a dark or black van, the driver got out went to the victim and then drove away, so tomorrow Steve and I will be going to York to find out what is happening. The victim is a George MacCrae, remember the list of nick names Mac was crossed out so perhaps the other one crossed out, Spider Webb, is also dead. Tomorrow the rest of you need to concentrate on all the counties around Yorkshire, except Peter, Ministry of Transport, how many Commer vans were made and how many are left? Steve, I will pick you up from home at 8am. Oh and Reg, a list of photographers in Doncaster, weddings or otherwise."

York

Renton picked up Steve and they set off for York, "I know this road quite well." Renton said. "Let's go via Tadcaster and stop for a quick cuppa and then on to the City of York."

They arrived in DI Bill Reynolds's office right on 11am.

After introducing Steve to DI Reynold, Renton said "So, the witness is a bit anti?"

"She feels that the constable that took the statement regarded her as a bit doddery, which she is. He took a good statement but he had to go over it several times so you can forget talking to her. It was a foggy night 8pm on Sunday 3rd February this year. She is walking her dog down Stockton Lane. Ahead but on the other pavement to her left is MacCrae staggering along drunk as a skunk and about 50 yards in front. She is aware that a dark van possibly black is somewhere behind her but parked with the engine running for some reason, she thought it was a taxi. MacCrae lives in Garden Street which you are familiar with I believe Ralph." He winked at Steve.

Renton said "My ex lived in Garden Street when I met her. Nice area though despite that."

"MacCrae, big chap, boozer, gambler, man about town, very well off, known by every bookie and publican in York and beyond. Likes to meet men in toilets to talk about horse racing. So MacCrae decides to cross over, next thing a dark van comes flying along and hits him with such force that he is catapulted to the other side of the road. Van stops and witness sees man dressed in dark clothing get out and go to MacCrae. She goes to the nearest house and asks them to call an ambulance. When she comes back onto the pavement, man and van have gone. She goes to MacCrae who is mumbling something and in his hand was this."

He opened a drawer on his desk and out of an evidence bag pulled a British Legion poppy with 1915 written on it and said "From all accounts you have one of these as well. This is exhibit BR/1. This was passed to the copper who took the statement from the ambulance driver. MacCrae died on the way to the hospital so it is registered as a hit and run, but eventually someone reads the post mortem report and the witness statement and decides "Oh my God could it be murder." And it lands on my desk. For some reason bearing in mind there is only one witness the powers that sit in judgement on the floor above decide to do a press release. Waste of time, Russians or maybe a little green man from Mars all the usual bullshit. Here is a copy of the post mortem. He sustained a broken arm, wrist and 3 ribs but died of a heart attack as he laid on the pavement."

Renton then told him about Miller and the crossing out of the nicknames.

"So we have a serial killer somewhere in the North, I won't say that to you know who." He pointed to the ceiling. "I have made an appointment for you to meet the housekeeper, Mrs. Ellis, at 2pm. She prefers to be called Miss MacCrae as she is the sister. Apparently Mr Ellis copped it in the war. So why don't we go to the canteen for some grub and then you can go to Garden Street."

The Housekeeper

Right on 2pm, Steve knocked on the door. It was opened by Mrs. Ellis, a smartly dressed woman in her sixties. Renton introduced himself and Steve and they showed their ID cards.

"It's a good thing someone rang me, I am going on holiday tonight and nearly finished packing." She showed them into the lounge and said "I will make a cuppa, you have come a fair way."

The two policemen waited in the lounge. Steve could hear the solemn tick of a grandfather clock. He looked around, they were surrounded by some very nice antique furniture.

Mrs. Ellis brought in a trolley and then put everything on a coffee table and sat opposite on an armchair. She said "Coffee in this pot, cream or milk and tea in this pot and some real shortbread from Scotland. Considering the distance you have come you have restored my faith in the police. I don't think the York police are up to much. Please call me Eileen."

Renton said "We are investigating a murder that took place in Doncaster and we think your brother and our victim knew each other. Do you mind if my colleague makes notes as we speak?"

"Of course not if it brings justice to my door."

"Can you tell us about George MacCrae from birth to his death?"

"We were both born in Edinburgh. George in 1896 and me 3 years later. Our parents were well off, owning a farm and a riding stables. Also, and as you can see from our furniture, our father dabbled in antiques but father had a stroke in 1907 so sold the farm, kept the riding stables and the family went into antiques in a big way, eventually selling the stables. We both went to private schools and learnt to ride and George was mad about horses. I eventually trained as a nurse. George was always restless and when war broke out in 1914 he enlisted in the Army Service Corps.

Needless to say father was not happy, he wanted George to be an officer. George went off to war ending up in Etaples. His letters were full of what he was doing and he was a sergeant in no time and in charge of several hundred horses. He came back from the war and joined the Metropolitan Police with his friends. By 1926 he was a police sergeant. He retired in 1950 as an Inspector, I think he had something to do with the mounted branch of course, more horses. He moved here to York and I was a widow so moved here to look after him, it was very convenient for both of us. Father had left us both a sizeable amount of money."

"George never married then?"

"Oh no, he wasn't a misogynist, nothing like that he just preferred the company of men. You said the chap who was murdered in Doncaster was a friend of George?"

"Yes. Leonard Miller."

"Oh my God how awful, not Dusty."

"Yes, did he come here at all?"

"He would come for the races and they would stay in a hotel and George would go to Doncaster."

"So when was the last time that George and Leonard met?"

"I think that would have been about 1960, in the summer."

"Do you know the names of any of his other friends?"

"Only their nicknames. It was always Spider Webb, Tug Wilson and their officer Tommo, oh and there was a Chalky White who was their cook."

Renton showed her the photograph of them paddling in the sea and said "Do you know the name of the one with the towels?"

"That's Eddy, his name was Edward, but I don't know his surname."

"What was Eddy's actual job in Etaples?"

"Well he was the cook's assistant, I know he was 15 in 1915, but he also helped out in the stables, George taught him to ride. Thinking about it now the cook was sergeant major Arthur White, Chalky, he took Eddy under his wing and looked after him. I think he also helped Spider in the bakery."

"Do you know where Eddy was from?"

"He was a Londoner, I think."

"Well thank you for all what you have told us. Here is my card and if you think of the actual names I would be most grateful if you give me a call."

In the car Steve said "Do you think she really does know their real names?"

"No," Renton said. "I think George was very secretive about his past life in the army and the police."

Commer Vans

Renton arrived at his usual time, checked his tray and then went down to the collators. Reg was talking to Austin and Frank. He said "Another homosexual was Mac, it sounds like. I don't think the sister quite realised how rampant he really was."

"Homosexuality," Frank said "was against Kings Regs and in those days. If you were caught out it was hard labour in the glasshouse, which may have been preferable to being shot at while you were knee deep in mud and shit."

Gradually everyone came in, made a drink and settled down. Renton then told them about the trip to York and the life and death of George MacCrae. He then beckoned to Reg for the cigar box. He laid out the photographs and said "have a look at this, they are for our eyes only." When everyone had looked at them he put them back in the cigar box and returned it to Reg.

Renton said "So we are now learning about life at Etaples and my distinct impression is that Eddy was used by them all for whatever job they needed doing but it would seem that he had a guardian with the cook, Chalky White. So over to Peter, what can you tell me about Commer vans?"

Peter said "They were originally produced in the 1950s and there were various versions and some were used by the military. I was given a telephone number of a chap in Hounslow who bought quite a few and then auctioned them off in job lots. Some went to Hong Kong, some to various parts of Asia and Germany. He was left with a few odd ones. I asked him to read out the names of those that were sold singly. He wasn't very happy so I said I would send the Mets round. He perked up and read the names out. One in particular stood out, the name on the cheque was William Morton, initials W.M., the same found on Miller's murder weapon. It was sold in 1959 and the address given was in Streatham. I checked with the Mets and the address had been knocked down and is now a block of 6 flats sandwiched between the shops."

"That's good work Peter, but something more pressing is to find the other three names on the list, Spider Webb, Tug Wilson and Tommo. To that end I think we need to contact collators in the counties around Yorkshire. Reg has prepared a list of the main places in each county and their collators. Steve and Tina you have got Lancashire and Merseyside, Dennis and Jack Lincolnshire and David and Peter Derbyshire. I will see you all at 5pm unless of course you find one of our names."

Just then Ted came in and said "I am now officially attached to this enquiry so what have you got for me?"

Renton said "We need to find out who Miller's colleagues were in the war, the people that worked in the Postal Section and also who joined the Metropolitan Police in 1918 and 19 from the army. I know it is a big ask but can you give it a go."

Ted said "Right, why don't I start at the Army Recruiting office." With that he was gone.

Jack said "He loves a mission."

Just then the collators telephone rang, Reg answered it. When he put the receiver down he said to Renton "That was Margery. Could you go and see the Chief, he would like you to meet a local called Walter Dobson."

Renton left.

Bayonet

Renton went into the Chief's office and he introduced him to Walter Benson "Walter is the chairman of our Joint Committee and also a local councillor. He suggested we have a press release which I did yesterday." They shook hands and sat down.

Benson said "How soon do you think you will have this serial killer behind bars then Inspector?"

Renton said "Detective Chief Inspector actually Mr Benson, but first we need to find out who the killer is. I am sure you appreciate that with the small amount of forensic evidence we have that we are in the early stages of this investigation. Plus the fact that Mr Miller was only killed 5 days ago AND the other murder was in February in York."

"Yes, yes I quite understand and I am sure the press release will help. It was my idea."

"The problem with a press release is that it ties up officers answering crank calls when they could be better used elsewhere."

The Chief could see that both Renton and Benson were getting a bit hot under the collar and said "Well I am glad that you two chaps have met and Ralph, I will let you get back to your chaps."

With that Renton went back to the incident room and told Frank about Benson.

Frank said "Benson is a pain in the backside, failed copper, only lasted 14 months then quit."

Renton was just about to leave when Steve came in and said "Just heard back from the Merseyside collators. Edward Webb, killed with a bayonet in Liverpool. Here is their DI's telephone number, it happened 1961, 5th November."

Renton went to his office and rang the telephone number. It rang a few times before a voice said "Hello Detective Inspector Robert Williams, how can I help?"

"Hello this is DCI Renton from Doncaster Constabulary, are you ok to talk?"

"Yes of course, our collator said one of your chaps had been trying to find if we had any retired police officers who had been murdered. His name was Edward Webb."

"Would it be ok for me to come over to see you about the case, I think our murder victim was a friend of yours?"

"Yes of course, be great to talk. Morning prayers will be finished by eleven so any time after that."

Renton put the receiver down and thought, it looks like we have found our 'Spider' Webb. He went to see the Chief. He saw Margery first and asked if Benson was still there. She said "No, thank God. I cannot stand that man, the sooner he goes the better. Do you know he comes in here, never makes an appointment and always says "I am here you can now announce me woman." What a pig."

Renton then went in and told the Chief about Liverpool.

Later at 5pm when everyone was assembled he told them about Edward Webb. He said to Ted "Did you have any luck with the Army?"

Ted said "Not a chance, we have got more chance of talking to General Haig's ghost. From the Met side I think they just didn't like him. Nothing more enlightening."

"Righto. Tomorrow, Steve and I will be going to Liverpool to see what we can learn there. Everyone else pair up and widen the search or cap comforter man to Armthorpe, Bentley, Sprotborough and Rossington. anywhere he might buy a cuppa, a sandwich and fuel. If we get back in time we will have a debrief at 5pm."

Liverpool

Renton picked up Steve and said "I think we will skirt round Manchester, maybe stop in Stockport for a cuppa. The DI said their morning prayers would be finished by eleven so we can get there easily by that time but have you heard the news? Apparently there has been some big train robbery thousands of pounds."

They arrived just after eleven and a constable took them to the DI. As they went through a uniformed superintendent who had been sitting down stood up and said "Ah at last."

Renton introduced himself and Steve.

The superintendent said "I have just spoken to your Chief of police we are more than willing to help but don't forget this is a two-way street and it is all about co-operation between us. He then walked out. The DI then saluted and said "Please sit down, sorry about that, he is a bit miffed because he was hoping to be the Chief here and has been pushed aside and because we are now no nearer to catching the killer than we were in 1961. Here is the file for you to see how it compares with your victim and this is the brute that did the job."

He produced the murder weapon.

Renton said "That is not a standard British bayonet."

Steve said "It looks more like a sword."

The DI said "No you are right our expert says it is Napoleonic. Apparently Nappy's bodyguard had these on the end of their muskets. As you can see the end is even serrated."

Renton said "Our victim was strangled, but had been tied up and gagged then strangled. Our pathologist thinks that the killer wanted to tell his victim something and then strangled him, untied him and then carried him into the gents toilet and plonked him on the porcelain having pulled his trousers down. Then jabbed the sharp end of an entrenching tool circa 1914 in his throat."

The DI said "Our victim was doped up or drugged and then had this brute shoved in his chest with such force that the blade sliced into his heart and out the back pinning him to the back of his wheelchair. Oh and he tied him to the chair first. The rope and gag were not at the scene. So perhaps he wanted to have a chat and tell him what he was going to do to him."

"Despite having different methods of killing, the talking to them smacks of revenge."

"Yes, because our victim was wheelchair bound the housekeeper would leave the back door open so he could wheel himself to the outside lavatory. Her theory was that the killer came in over a couple of days using some sort of ruse to talk to him. Then drug him sufficiently to tie him up. Then kill him."

Renton then told him about the hit and run and the fact that Miller, MacCrae and Webb had all been in the war together and the police. And that there were two others who may still be alive.

The DI said "I have made an appointment for you to see his housekeeper for 1.30pm. I thought maybe you would like a spot of lunch here in our canteen and then go and see her."

After lunch the DI produced a map and said "She lives here in Aigburth Vale near Sefton Park and we are here." He pointed on the map. "Keep the map."

Renton said "I understand there was a press release."

"Yes, the uniform that was in here earlier did that. The problem is that scousers think that talking to the police is grassing. They don't know the difference between grassing someone up for nicking sweets from Woolworths or murder."

"Was he ever married and was he a Freemason?"

"No to the first and yes to the Lodge."

"Righto thank you. And I will keep you informed."

Mrs Phillips

Renton knocked on the door. It was opened by a lady in her fifties. She said "The policemen from Doncaster I presume."

As he pulled out his ID card Renton said "How do you know that Mrs Phillips?"

She said "I can see Doncaster Borough Police on that folder your young colleague is holding."

"You should be a detective."

"Yes I reckon I could do a better job than the Liverpool City Police, anyway come in and have a cuppa."

They went through to the kitchen and she said "You have come a fair way I must say, tea or coffee?"

Renton said "Coffee is fine for both of us."

He then watched her go through what his Aunt Alice said was "The Northern Visitors Routine." She brought out a milk jug and sugar bowl both covered with knitted doilies edged with imitation pearls. She made a pot of tea for herself and a flask of black coffee for them. Next out came the cake tin.

She said "I am forgetting my manners, would you like a sandwich, I have some lovely cheese and just bought some nice Yorkshire ham."

Renton said "Oh the cake is fine, we have had lunch at the police station, but thank you."

With that she gave them each a whopping slice of fruit cake accompanied with a slice of cheese.

She said "Some might say this is a poor man's pudding but us Northern folk like a nice piece of crumbly Lancashire cheese with our fruit cake, it aids the tummy with its digestion."

After a bit of cake and cheese Renton had a sip of his coffee and said "Are you related to Mr. Webb?"

"Good heavens no I am his live in housekeeper come carer I suppose, I couldn't tell you what my official title is. I have my own bedroom and since his stroke Edward was sleeping in the lounge, it was easier for him to use the toilet out in the garden. You do know he was in a wheel chair?"

"Yes, Inspector Williams filled us in on the details of his murder."

"Yes, nice chap. About the only one."

"He tells me you have a theory about Edward's death?"

"Yes. You see Edward liked to keep the back door open, to get to the privy but also he was a bit of a fresh air type. Also after the stroke we had doctors and a nurse coming so it was more convenient for him really. Occasionally the neighbours would come in but that tailed off. I think the killer watched the address and came in a couple of times. Edward said he had had someone from the military asking him if he had been approached about a First World War pension which I know is rubbish because he had tried to get one in the past."

"Did he describe this man?"

"Big feller, in a blazer reminded him of what the officers wore when they were day off. Posh accent, smelt of cigars. Have you seen the post mortem report?"

Renton said "I hope you don't mind me saying this but you seem very knowledgable about police work."

"Yes, both Edward and I were very fond of crime novels. I first met Edward in 1935 when he transferred to Liverpool, I was then a typist in the police station. My husband was killed in the war in 1942. Edward retired in 1945 and suggested I earn a better wage by being his housekeeper and I have been here ever since."

"When did he have the stroke?"

"That was early January 1958. He took it very badly at first. It was mainly his left side but I encouraged him to fight back and he did. It was my idea to get the wheelchair and my cousin who is a carpenter built it for him nice and solid so he could lever himself out to get in the toilet. Also I would take him out in it when the weather was nice."

"Do you mind if Steve makes a few notes and can you tell us about Edward?"

"Yes, please do. Well, as a baby he was dumped outside the police station and found by PC Webb so he got that as his surname. There was a note in the box he was in saying Edward born 3rd June and that was in 1890. He was taken to the orphanage and taught by the nuns. It was a tough life and the girls from an early age would go into domestic service and the boys were trained as plumbers or carpenters but Edward was trained as a baker. Another piece of cake young man?" She passed Steve another wedge of fruit cake.

"He then joined the army?" Renton asked.

"Yes. By that time he was 24 and a master baker with credentials. He was put in the Army Service Corps and posted to somewhere in the south of England turning out vast amounts of bread for our boys in France. By the time he was posted to France he was a sergeant and a bit later on became a sergeant major I think."

"Do the names Tommo or Tug Wilson or Chalky White mean anything to you?"

"Tommo was their officer, a bit of a bully and a big mate of a Dusty Miller. Ernest Wilson was something to do with the stables and let me see,

Arthur White was a sergeant major in charge of cooking for them all and the wounded and medical staff. He looked after the kid Eddy."

"Can you tell us about Eddy?"

"Yes he was the dogsbody, running errands, working in the stables and Edward used him in the bakery occasionally. I think he had a very busy life. His name was William Edward Horton or maybe Morton."

Renton said "Can Steve just take a statement from you about their real names?"

When the statement was done Renton said "So after army service, Edward joined the police?"

"Yes, Thomas the officer who had connections in London and quite a bit of money fixed it for them all to join the police in London. When Edward retired he had some savings and had a bakery here in Liverpool but in 1955 he and his business partner sold up."

"Do you know what happened to Eddy, did he join the police?

"Oh no he went back to London and worked in his father's business."

"Do you know what that was?"

"No."

"So all the others joined the police?"

"No not all. Arthur White worked for Eddy's parents and then I think he became a cook somewhere in the North of England."

"Did Edward never marry?"

"No, he said the only two women he trusted was his accountant and me. He was a man's man, stayed in touch with his police friend's right up to his stroke."

"Do you have anything from his past?"

She went into the lounge and returned with a familiar looking brown envelope and a bayonet.

"A British bayonet?" said Renton.

"Yes, he had it through the war and used it to defend himself against a thief in his bakery shop." She gave the envelope to Renton.

He pulled out a birthday card that said "Happy 71st from Eddy." Also in there was the familiar poppy with "1915 to 1918" written on it.

Renton said "Did he have a place to go to be with his thoughts?"

"Church, Methodist not Catholic right up to his stroke, then he didn't want to meet anyone he knew." She pulled a letter out of a drawer and gave it to Renton. He read "Edward thank you for your generous donation of 200 hundred pounds. I hope you find peace in your retirement". It was dated June 1954. It was signed Matthew and at the top of the letter was Battersea Methodist Church.

Renton said "Do you know his surname?" he pointed to Matthew.

"No but he was a lay preacher and a medic during the war I think. I would imagine he knew all of Edward's friends."

Renton said "Well thank you for all of this, I will always have cheese from now on when I eat fruit cake. Here is my card and if you should remember any detail don't hesitate to ring me. Both DI Williams and I will keep you up to date."

As Renton drove back to Doncaster Steve said "What a break William Edward Horton or Morton. It's got to be Morton, the initials on the spade WM."

Renton said "Yes, we need to find this lay preacher and I know just the man."

Steve said "I can't imagine that Eddy sent that card, I mean he would be about 61 then, too old to drive a bayonet through Edward Webb's chest, let alone kill old Maungy Miller and carry him down those steps to the toilets. I can't see him doing the hit and run on George MacCrae either."

"Yes Steve, I think someone is acting for him."

When they arrived back it was just on 6pm. Everyone had gone home except Reg. Renton told him about Matthew and the Battersea Methodist Church and asked him to get on that first thing in the morning.

15

Day Seven of the Investigation

Renton arrived at his usual time and looked at his desk calendar. Saturday 10th August 1963, the seventh day of the investigation. Frank came in and said "Penny for your thoughts."

Renton said "We found out yesterday that Eddy is William Eddy Morton. There's a preacher at Battersea Methodist Church who was a lay preacher at Etaples and probably knew Eddy and his tormentors. Let's get a coffee while I write up my diary."

They went into the collators and found Reg making a cuppa. He made Renton a black coffee and then he went into the incident room to write up his diary as the rest of the team drifted in. By 9.30 everyone was there except Frank who was at morning prayers.

Reg said "Before you start the Chief gave out a small item to the press while you were in Liverpool. That was at 10am. By 11.30am the crank calls had started and so far they have had nearly 20. There is a bobby, PC Colin Turton, who is sitting with Daisy the operator taking the calls and making notes."

Renton said "Thanks for that Reg, so Steve read out the statements from yesterday."

Afterwards Renton said "With the initials WM on the spade I think we can safely say that it is William Morton not Horton."

Peter put his hand up.

Renton said "Yes Peter I know what you are going to say, about the Commer and the address in London of the buyer of a Commer. Here we are into the seventh day of the investigation and I think we are doing well but do we think it is possible for a 61 year old man to push this bayonet." He put down the photograph of the French bayonet on the table. "Into the chest of a man, through the back with such force and venom to pin him to the back of his wheelchair. Also carry Miller down to the toilets. I think this is cap comforter man, described as well built, 6 foot and in his forties so someone is being paid to do the killing or a relative, maybe a son. Steve, tell us all the housekeeper's statement."

Steve then explained what Mrs Phillips had said.

Renton said "I think that is exactly what happened to Webb. The post mortem report said that he had a sedative in his system which rendered him sleepy. Why tie up a man in a wheelchair and gag him? To tell him why he was going to die, just like Miller. So what were you lot doing while we were enjoying fruit cake with cheese?"

David said "We went to the various areas you gave us and came up with nothing, but Jack and Dennis found out something"

16

The Pig Man

Jack said "After we had scoured the mining villages for cap comforter man, Dennis and I went into Dick's Diner just as he was getting ready to close up. However he had Bernie Hopwood in, known locally as the pig man. He goes around collecting vegetable scraps which he feeds to his pigs and in turn sells his meat cheaply. The bacon and sausages in the Diner are from Bernie's pigs, absolute quality. He has a brown battered Commer van which you can smell before you see him so we get talking about Commer vans and give him the description of our man."

Dennis said "He said he was over Campsall on Tuesday and saw a man with that description changing the tyre on a red Rover. So Bernie being a nosy sort goes over and asks him if he wants a hand. Man gets up and said he wouldn't mind a light and produces a cigar the size of a telegraph pole and offers Bernie one. Bernie says to us "a bit strange wearing a green cap comforter in this weather". He also said to us that it seemed a bit weird that a mechanic would be smoking expensive cigars and smelt of that poncey aftershave that the officers in the war used. Bernie mentions what a nice car, must have cost a few bob. Our man says it belongs to his uncle and he takes him out for a drive now and then."

Renton said "Where is Campsall?"

Jack said "Not far, seven miles or to Askern."

Renton said "For the rest of today and tomorrow, all of you off to Campsall and go where he would go for petrol, a sandwich and if his uncle owns a new Rover then perhaps he has a big house." As he finished talking he saw Reg giving him a thumb's up. He went to his desk and said "Something good?"

Reg said "Oh yes. Matthew Armstrong is now retired from the church and lives in South Norwood. They gave me his telephone number. This evening he is driving to Filey with his wife, which is on the east coast, about 60 miles from here, he has a caravan there. I explained about Miller and Webb and that we were trying to trace Wilson and someone called Tommo who may still be alive. He said Tommo is Thomas Bond. He is coming here for 3pm tomorrow so you will have plenty of time for your roast in the Red Lion."

Frank said "More crank calls too. One of the first was the Harris family from Armthorpe."

"Enlighten me presumably one of our more colourful characters."

Jack said "William Henson Harris known to all as Billy. Born 1898, enlisted in 1915 to get away from the black hole. Being only 5 foot 4 inches he ends up in a tunnelling company with some Aussies. Does that for a while then gets trench foot, scabies and the pox allegedly. Anyway he gets invalided out with a very small pension which he ekes out by breaking into people's homes. 1920 Harold, his son, is born, he bought it on D-Day but not before he fathers the next generation, another Billy, born 1942. Now a part-time miner but also a car thief. He in turn has fathered another Billy born 1958. But it is the first Billy who rings in and wants to confess. He confessed to a murder in Bradford way back. He got a thumping for his troubles then kicked out and tried to sue Bradford Constabulary for assault and wrongful arrest."

"Why us?" Renton said.

17

Matthew Armstrong

Renton arrived at 9am and briefly saw Frank who was going to prayers. He checked his tray and found a couple of supplements about the latest criminal trials that had taken place recently. He went down to the collators, made himself a coffee and said to Reg "Did David ever get a reply from the Ministry of Defence about Miller?"

Reg looked through his reports file and said "He did. It was dated 7th August, you was in York. It basically said what Doris Jenkins told you about his life."

Renton said "I take it the troops had no luck yesterday after I left?"

"No, nothing."

"Righto, I am going home for a bath. Shouldn't you be day off today?"

"Yes but Mrs P has organised a small tea party come luncheon for her WI colleagues so sandwiches and a bit of radio 3 is my Sunday and I have some cards to type up."

Renton went to the Red Lion and had a very nice roast lamb, Frank had the roast beef. By 2pm they were back in the station. Steve was there ready for the interview. To one side Renton said to Frank, "What do you think if we make Steve an acting DS from now on?"

Frank said "Yes I think he will make the grade."

"Especially when you get DI next year?"

"Oh I don't know about that."

Renton said "You know Johnny Martin is on about emigrating to Australia?"

Frank nodded. "Yes, but will he do it? He comes from a big family and they are spread around Donny. He has 3 sisters and 3 brothers and they are all married with kids."

"A virile dad by the sound of it. Because all the troops are out and about, I think we will bring Armstrong into the incident room away from that awful broom cupboard that is supposed to be an interview room. Reg is covering up the photos and other material. "

Frank said "They have nearly finished the new witness-come-interview room in the front office."

3pm. Steve brought Matthew Armstrong through to the incident room and introduced him to Renton, Frank and Reg. He then made him a mug of strong tea, no milk or sugar.

Renton said "Do you mind if Steve makes some notes and we may need to take a statement?"

Matthew said. "No, not at all."

Renton said "I am told that you served at Etaples, can you tell us in what capacity?"

"I enlisted as a medic in the RAMC, my father was a doctor and I was training to be doctor but the war cut that short. Because of that I became a sergeant medic and eventually a quarter master sergeant in charge of all the medicines, bandages and all the paraphernalia that goes with nursing. I also had to go to the stores regularly to get the supplies and that is where I met that bunch of creatures."

"You don't sound very impressed by them?"

"Apart from Eddy and Chalky White they were skivers. I mean they did their jobs but lived off what they could scrounge."

"So you knew Leonard Miller?"

"Yes."

"Edward Webb?"

"Unfortunately."

"George MacCrae?"

"Again unfortunately."

"Ernest Wilson?"

"Loathsome."

"Finally, Thomas Bond?"

"Yes he was the officer in charge of that lot, Lieutenant and then Captain. I mean he was in charge of the various departments that they worked in. He and Miller were lovers."

"Tell us about Eddy and Chalky White?"

"First of all, I must say that those others used Eddy as a messenger boy and orderly and made his war hell but he bore it all magnificently. His guardian was Chalky, Arthur White, he was the sergeant major in charge of all the cooks and cooking in that particular area and fortunately Eddy was billeted in a tent with the cooks. I tried to help, Bond and his gang knew that if they overstepped the mark then Chalky and I would blow their world apart. Eddy's full name was William Edward Morton and a lovely, honest lad he was. I had the privilege of knowing him until he died."

Renton shot a look to Frank.

Matthew said "Have I said something wrong."

"Oh no." Renton said. "Our killer has killed Miller here in Doncaster, Webb in Liverpool and MacCrae in York in the last 2 years. He knew of them and we thought it might be Eddy despite now being in his sixties."

"I conducted Eddy's funeral service, so believe me he died before the killings started.

"So can we safely say that the gang were all homosexuals? A possible motive?"

"Bond, Miller and Macrae certainly. I think MacCrae and Wilson had something going in the stables. Bond and Wilson were bisexual but I don't think your killer killed them because of that. I think he was exacting revenge for the way they treated young Eddy during the war. Bearing in mind he was just 14 when he arrived at Etaples."

Renton said "Let's have a drink and Reg, you can bring out that box of biscuits you have been hiding. But first I would like Steve to take a statement from you naming all the parties we have just talked about."

18

Armstrong Part 2

Steve took Matthew to the toilet and Frank said to Renton "We need him to tell us who the killer is, we just need to ask the right questions."

"Yes, I was thinking that."

Having had another drink and some of Reg's cherished biscuits, a brief statement was taken and Renton said "Can you tell us what you know about Eddy's life and death?"

"He was born on 7th June 1900 to Horace and Dandy Morton. They owned a cleaning company, offices and shops. He enlisted and passed the recruiting board somehow just before Christmas. Within weeks of being at the Front they found out he was too young because his mum had written to him and one of his comrades read the letter. So he was posted to Etaples in the postal section where he was under Miller. Sadistic creature Miller was, he made him dig a latrine trench with his spade, his entrenching tool. Bond did eventually put a stop to it. Before they went on one of their trips to Paris, Miller gave him instruction's to dig another. Macrae and Wilson, had him mucking out the stables. Wilson a couple of times made him pick up the manure with his hands and one day tried to get him to eat some of it but the farriers put a stop to that."

"What about Webb, he was a baker?"

"Yes they had him doing the deliveries to and from the cookhouse and food from the bakery. Webb had a bayonet and his trick was to do that thing where you throw it so it lands next to your foot and you gradually stretch out almost doing the splits, he actually caught William on the ankle and he had to have a couple of stitches. He also liked to creep up on him and threaten him with the knife saying "You were lucky that time I could have been a German.""

Renton said "I would like Steve to take another statement with you just describing what they did to William."

20 minutes later Renton showed Matthew the card with the lines through the names and said "Do you know where Wilson and Bond are now?"

"Wilson was born in Pontefract, he had a broad Yorkshire accent. I think his parents moved to London when he was in the police. Bond was a Londoner and came from a very well to do family. I know his brother Robert Bond was some sort of industrialist. Every month he sent his brother a box of those huge cigars that Churchill smokes."

"If they were going off for little trips, how did they stay at Etaples?"

"They ran the stores like clockwork and the stables. The Army Service Corps was a massive operation delivering everything a soldier needed from bread to bullets. Bond and his gang were very efficient but very corrupt."

"Did you ever see them bullying him or sexually abusing him?"

"Only once when it was the bayonet thing because of William having medical treatment. MacCrae did try it on with Eddy in the stables but the farriers put a stop to that, despite MacCrae being a big chap you don't take on a farrier with a hammer in his hand."

"You said they were corrupt."

"The black market is everywhere, even in the trenches. Soldiers coming in wounded were stripped, washed and repaired. Their equipment and rifles, bayonets everything was sorted out, fixed and then used as replacement but their souvenirs, such as German helmets, the ones with a spike on top, revolvers, medals and so on was taken by the gang and then either sold or shipped back to the industrialist brother's warehouse."

"So what happened to Eddy at the end of the war?"

"Arthur White, the cook, had a brother who was an officer who had been badly wounded at Mons and when he recovered he ended up working for the Minister of War in Whitehall, so with his help we managed to get Eddy demobbed in 1918, just before his eighteenth birthday. Bond and the gang weren't happy and they threatened to do Arthur and me. So I told them that we had sent a letter to Arthur's brother on the understanding that should anything untoward happen to us he would inform the Ministry about their homosexual and criminal activities."

"So what happened to Arthur and Eddy after the war?"

"Arthur worked for Eddy's parents for a while and then came up North and got a cooking job. Eddy went back into the family business. In the meantime I had been ordained and had great pleasure in marrying Eddy to his childhood sweetheart and also christening their son Michael."

"So when was Michael born and what happened to him?"

"By then it was 1921. Eddy's parents, Horace and Dandy, had built up a very successful business and Eddy continued with that. Michael had a very good private education and excelled in languages and sports. Along came the second war and he enlisted in the Royal marines but somewhere along the line he ended up in SOE, Special Operations Executive. When I asked him about it he just tapped his nose. During the blitz their shop was bombed and his mum was killed and Eddy was very badly hurt. He died in 1956. Before he died he gave me a package and said that when he had died to give it to Michael."

Renton said "Did you give him the package?

"Yes."

"Do you know what was in it?"

"I think photographs, memorabilia from the war and a diary about William's life."

"So after the war did Michael continue with the business in London?"

"After the war he continued working with some business overseas, Eddy had slimmed down the business and Michael helped out when he was in London. I never asked what he did with his own business and then about 6 weeks after the funeral he came to me and said he was selling the business, and his lovely house in Dulwich. I then asked him what he was doing work wise and he said because of his contacts abroad he was doing an import/export business."

"Has he stayed in touch?"

"I saw him in 1958, Christmas he came to our church service and gave me some money for the church and he gave me enough money to buy the caravan in Filey. He said for looking after his dad during the war. The next time was in 1960 or maybe 61. He turned up in a lovely car, a bright red Rover, very posh. He said the business was doing well, but I think he was doing some secret agent stuff. I asked him what was in the package I had given him and he said stuff from the war, medals, photographs and some newspaper cuttings and a diary that his dad had kept from the war and into peacetime."

Renton said "Just between you and me Matthew, I think Michael is our killer and avenging his father for what he went through in the war?"

Matthew said "I hope you are wrong. I have to say I never saw Michael ever lose his temper or show any aggression as long as I have known him."

Renton said "Here is my card and if he does get in touch with you I would be obliged if you contacted me."

As he walked out Matthew said "I have just had a thought I think Arthur White found work somewhere in North Yorkshire."

After he had gone Renton said to the others "I think Morton is our man and I reckon he has a base in London but is operating from somewhere near here."

Everyone else came back from their enquiries, made a drink and settled down. Renton said "So what have you got for me?"

David said "Not a thing, no Rover or Commer or cap comforter man."

Renton then told them about the conversation with Matthew Armstrong. He then said "Frank you can circulate the Rover and the Commer throughout the 3 Ridings again. I will contact my counterparts in the counties around Yorkshire and we need to find Arthur White the cook in North Yorkshire somewhere, so make up your pocket books and I will see you all tomorrow."

19

Yorkshire

Renton arrived at his usual time and then went to see Margery to ask if he could see the Chief before morning prayers. She called the Chief and he said "Now be good to see him."

Renton then went in and explained what Matthew Armstrong had told him about the Morton family. The Chief said he was very pleased the way the investigation was going and together they formed a new strategy.

Later Renton went down to the incident room. Once everyone had a drink he said "I have just seen the Chief and this is what is going to happen. David, I want you to go round North Yorkshire, York, Ripon and Selby and anywhere you might find a cook, and look for Arthur White, we have only his name. That is your task for today. Now for you others Frank will outline what we want."

Frank said. "You are all going out to different areas to sit and watch for our man and either the Commer or a red Rover. Try and set up in a market or any sort of hub.

"Ted, you head northwards for Sherburn in Elmet. Dennis, head west towards Rawmarsh. Jack, go south to Worksop and lastly Tina and me will go east to Blyton. We have four DOs coming to help out so grab one of them as a partner if you don't have one. Out all day, back here for 6pm. That's it. Here are the car keys for your unmarked cars."

Renton said "We are now fairly sure that the killer is Michael Morton, the son of Eddy. Also he worked for the SOE during the war and is probably still connected to a secret service so if you do apprehend him then take no chances. Good luck out there."

Renton then said "Peter, to my office it is time for your yearly assessment."

In his office Renton said "I am really pleased with the way you have worked with your colleagues, I know DI Johnny Martin is also pleased with your work. I notice that you type your reports which is excellent, do you think you could teach Jack? His handwriting is awful. Is there anything that you are looking towards in your future?"

"Well sir, I would like to get into the work that Ink and Blot do."

"Well, they are designated officers. I am pretty sure that we know who the murderer is so I will release you from this murder for 2 weeks. I know Blot has just started a holiday and Ink is not far from retirement so I will ring and let him know what is happening. Good luck."

Renton then returned to his office to mark up some files that had been passed to him from Chief Inspector Fox. He was just thinking about a coffee when his telephone rang. He answered it and said. "Detective Chief Inspector Renton, how may I help you?"

"Very professional I thought Ralph." It was Bill Reynolds, the DI from York who had told Renton about George MacCrae's hit and run.

"Bill, how are you? I hope you are wading through some files like me." He then told him what Matthew Armstrong had said about Eddy and his son Michael.

"That is quality. so you have the name of your man. Do you want some more good news?"

"You have arrested him."

"No not quite. I heard you were looking for an Arthur White and I think I might have tracked him down."

"That is really good news."

"To cut a long story short, I took the wife to a posh hotel in York for her birthday. When we had finished the chef brought out a mini birthday cake for Anne. On the off chance, I asked him if he knew of a chef or cook called Arthur White. Bugger me but he had been the chef in that very hotel, although then he went by Chef Pierre."

"Have you spoken to him?"

"No, apparently he came into some money and bought a flat when he retired in 1955. I had a word with a friend in the newspapers and he had a look at the local obituary from 1955 to now, no sign of White having died.
"

"I need to find that flat."

"Leave it with me. I will have a word with our community bobbies who cover York and far and wide."

"Thanks Bill you have made my day."

Renton then went downstairs made a coffee and told Reg what Bill Reynolds had said.

Reg said "That is great news. If Morton lobbed some money to Armstrong to say thank you for looking after dad then perhaps that is how White got his cash. Last night I went to choir practice and one of our tenors who is in his eighties and I were discussing how to track people down and he said what about the GRO, which he informed me is the General Records Office. They collate all the records of births deaths and marriages for England and Wales. He gave me the number which I have rung, mentioning his name. They said they can do a check for people but would need authorisation from our Chief. Here is the number."

"Righto, here I go."

20

GRO

Thirty minutes later Renton returned to Reg. "When you ring the GRO quote this number with our station code and me as the Officer in Charge. No messing by the Chief, rang the Attorney General straight away."

Reg rang them, quoted the code and gave Renton as the OIC. Then gave them the names of Bond, Wilson and White with first names and an approximate date of birth and where.

One hour late a GRO secretary rang back and Reg scribbled furiously on his notepad.

He said "Thomas Bond born 1st January 1890 in Dalousie, India. 1923 married Winifred Dobson registered in York. She was born on 17th March 1885 in Kensington. She died 9th September 1955 in York. Next up Ernest Wilson born 5th September 1890 registered in Pontefract. Now for Arthur White born 3rd October also 1890, very popular year, registered in Bradford. No sign of marriage for Wilson or White. No registration of death."

"Interesting she died in York when the races were on. If you had a few bob coming to the races where would you stay Reg."

"The Danum, I shall ring my contact." With that he rang the hotel and asked if anyone remembered the lady Winifred Bond who died at the races.

Twenty minutes later his telephone rang and after a conversation he put the receiver down.

"Yes, she and her husband were staying there in the Emperor's suite. Very expensive. They booked in on the 21st August for 3 weeks, however that was cut short by her death and here is their address in York. Apparently she was a large lady and very fond of champagne which she had every morning for breakfast. She had backed the big winner of the day and dropped dead with a heart attack.

Renton then rang Bill Reynolds and asked him to check the address.

Fifteen minutes later he said "The Bonds did live at that address but he sold the house to some developer who knocked it down and built a house to his own liking. Bond was a widower at this stage and told the man that he decided to go on a world cruise, but didn't give a further address."

Renton said to Reg "I thought we were on to a winner there."

Everyone returned from there endeavours with no success.

Renton said "Tomorrow, David and Tina see if White had any relatives in Bradford. Dennis and Jack to Pontefract, see if Wilson had any there and as for the rest of you, thank you for your efforts. I will be in the Red Lion for 6pm and the wallet will be open for 10 minutes."

Renton said to Frank "Are we ever going to find Wilson and Bond?"

Little did he know that within a month he would meet Wilson.

21

Knaresborough

Renton arrived at his desk at the usual time and noted that it was Thursday 15th August 1963, he also noted that he had extra files to approve. While he was on the murder it was the consensus that Chief Inspector Fox would be approving the files. However, his argument was that they were CID files and should be approved by a senior CID officer not by uniform who had enough to do. Frank said that Fox had always been a duck shoveller in every rank from sergeant.

Just as Renton started looking at the files, his telephone rang. Instinctively he looked at his watch, 9.20am. It was Bill Reynolds, he sounded excited.

"Our local bobbies have come up trumps, they have found Arthur White. He owns a cafe by the riverside in Knaresborough and lives above it."

"What's Knaresborough all about?"

"It's where senior police officers go to retire or coppers take their mistresses for a weekend. The cafe is where you go for a cup of tea and a scone and pretend it's the Ritz."

"So how did you find him?"

"I went back to the hotel and saw the chef. He was a bit reluctant at first but I said White might be on the hit list. He thought he might be in Knaresborough so I contacted the area sergeant and Bob's your uncle he came up with the cafe. Local bobby knows him says he's a nice chap. So I rang him up using my official tone and asked him outright if he knew a Michael Morton and his dad Eddy. He said he remembered Michel being born. He was a bit off to start with but when I said I was ringing as part of a murder enquiry he was more amenable. I told him you would like to have a chat, so he said come tomorrow for 2pm."

"Excellent. Thank you Bill, I owe you one."

Renton went down to the incident room and as he made a coffee he told Reg about the phone call. Then said "Have you ever been to Knaresborough?"

"Oh yes in our courting days by tandem. Tea and cakes by the river, very pleasant."

"Steve and I will be going there tomorrow."

Thirty minutes later Frank came in "Bloody morning prayers. That doubting bloody Thomas Walter Benson was there. Going on about Miller with "My brothers in the lodge want to know when you are going to catch the killer." I thought the Chief was going to punch him. He said "It's only been 12 days since your brother was found dead. I think our team are doing a wonderful job, so if you are not satisfied Walter then you get your brothers in the lodge to find the bloody killer." He was steaming. Benson left with his tail between his legs."

Renton said "I have just found out that Arthur White has a cafe in Knaresborough by the river."

Frank said "The River Nidd then."

"Really, what a geographer you are, what is on the menu today would you say at the Diner?"

"Oh one of my favourites toad in the hole with that lovely gravy, maybe even roast potatoes."

"Let's go, I'm starving."

By 5pm everyone was in the incident room.

Renton told them about Arthur White and said to Steve. "See you tomorrow morning at the usual time and then it's off to tea and scones by the river."

22

Arthur White

Renton picked up Steve at the usual time and said. "I think the A1 via Boston Spa, a little break in this glorious morning."

Steve said. "You're in a good mood this morning sir."

"I am always in a good mood Steve, I am the eternal optimist. Almost 2 weeks since our murder and already we have solved it for Liverpool and York and for us. The preacher gave us quite a bit and now I am hoping Chalky will give us some more leading to the arrest of Michael Morton."

After the tea break in Boston Spa they were driving through the lovely countryside of North Yorkshire and soon came the road sign pointing the way to Knaresborough. At 1pm they found a parking space and having had a quick look around arrived at the cafe. As they stood outside a young waitress was clearing a table and said "We will be closing very soon."

Renton said "That's all ok we are here to see Mr. White."

Several minutes later Arthur White came out. Renton introduced Steve and himself and they showed their ID cards.

White said "Fancy a coffee?" He led them into the cafe and said to the waitress "Jean can you put up the closed sign and call it a day. I'll wash up. I'm just making these chaps a cuppa."

After she had gone, he locked the door and said. "That will be all round the neighbourhood now two coppers having coffee in the cafe."

He produced a flask of coffee and some small cupcakes. "Tuck in, and call me Arthur, I understand you want to talk about the war and young Eddy."

"Well yes." Renton said. "We are investigating a murder in Doncaster of Leonard Miller, I think you knew him?"

"So, Dusty is stoking the fires of hell. Good riddance."

"Also murdered in the last 2 years were George MacCrae in York and Edward Webb in Liverpool."

"Well, well if God could cast his net. Just the other two to go, Wilson and Bond."

"You didn't like them?"

"Didn't like them is an understatement, they picked on Eddy until the end of 1915 although me and my cooks and the farriers put an end to the worst of it."

"Did you see them bullying Eddy?"

"MacCrae tried to rape him in the stables with Wilson in attendance waiting his turn, but the farriers stopped that and beat them up. They reported it to Captain bloody fancy Bond for all the good it did. All of them were bloody homos and stuck together. From then Eddy only worked in the stables when the farriers were there. The rest of the time he was with me and my lads. He was also billeted with us."

"What about Miller and Webb?"

"Miller was Bond's bum chum, thick as thieves, they were running the black market as well. Miller went out of his way to pick on the boy but from 1916 he eased off but only because he was a bloody coward. As for Webb he was in the closet too. He had a hunting knife on his belt, he was a bloody baker for God's sake who did he think he was Davy Crockett? He also had a bayonet which he tormented Eddy with."

"I have spoken to Matthew Armstrong and he said between you and him, you managed to get Eddy demobbed early."

"Yes, well, if he had been 18 they would have kept him on but because he was under 18 we managed to get him away early. My brother who was a major in the War office fixed it. You should have seen Bond and his cronies' faces when they found out he had gone. MacCrae and Wilson came looking for me but backed off, I am quite handy with a 3-foot ladle.

MacCrae's face was a picture and so was his uniform covered in tomato soup."

"So when you were demobbed, what did you do?"

"Eddy's dad Horace asked me if I would stay with them and work in the cleaning business, which I did. I did all the cooking. Dandy, Eddy's mum, loved cheesecake and I was quite good at that. It was a relief to have a job because thousands of lads would be coming back looking for jobs. When Michael arrived I thought it was time to go. Horace had a trade magazine and there was a vacancy for a pastry chef in a hotel in York and being a Yorkshireman I thought it was a good omen so I applied for the job. Horace gave me a reference and I got the job. Eventually I became the head chef, ha ha, Chef Pierre."

"Did you ever see Bond and his cronies again?"

"In 1935 Michael came up for 2 weeks in the summer and worked in the hotel, we did a bit of hiking and fishing and he had grown. Very quick on the uptake in the kitchen and very bright but in 1936 he came for a month in the summer. The owner of the hotel didn't have any children and took a shine to Michael, so he worked in the kitchen from 4pm to midnight which was my usual shift and did a bit of waitering. He was brilliant at languages so one night he would have a French accent, the next a German and the following night Spanish and got a few tips, especially from the women, he was a good-looking lad. The passage that led into the dining room has a one way window so we could look in and see the diners. I often went and looked just to keep an eye on things. One Saturday night we were really busy, York races had been busy, and a few of the punters were staying in the hotel. I looked in and I couldn't believe my eyes. Sitting at a table was Bond, Miller, Webb and Wilson. By this time they were over the meal but getting stuck into the brandy and champagne. I made shortbread for the waiters so put some on a tray and said to Michael to put on a bow tie and take the tray to the four men in suits on the end table and have a good look at them. He went out and put the tray down. I could hear him doing the French accent. I could see that filthy pervert Miller looking him up and down. He came back in the kitchen and I said "Those four men made your dad's life hell in the war." He clenched his fists and said "One day we might meet again.""

"I won't beat about the bush Arthur but I think Michael is fulfilling that wish and bumping them off."

"Good riddance I say, what about the other two?"

"We are trying to track them down now."

"The next day I had a look at the register and Bond had given an address in York, Webb was Liverpool I think, but I couldn't find the other two."

"Have you seen Michael since those days?"

"I saw him at his dad's funeral. I told him where I was living and a couple of months later he came to see me and said he had sold the business and that lovely house in Dulwich. He gave me a cheque for £5,000, I was stunned and said it was from Eddy. I asked him what he was up to and he said through his contacts in the war he had an import export business. The last time I saw him was this February. He must be doing well he had a lovely car."

"Do you know what he did in the war?"

"Matt said he had joined the Royal marines and was working with the French Resistance."

"Righto. I would like Steve here to take a small statement relating to what you knew had happened to William from Bond and his cronies."

Twenty minutes later, statement taken and signed, Renton said "Do you have an idea where Bond or Wilson might be living?"

"Wilson is from Yorkshire so he might be back here and Bond would have been near to his bum chum Miller I would think."

On the way back to Doncaster Steve said "Do you think he knows where Morton is?"

"He was a father to Eddy in the war, so it's possibly they are in touch. I will have a word with Bill asking the local police to keep an eye out for the Rover or the van."

Death in the Stables

It was Sunday 8th September 1963. Renton was sitting at his desk with the usual files waiting for his approval. Just over 3 weeks ago he had seen Arthur White and felt that at last they were getting nearer to arresting their killer. He had seen the Chief and told him about Morton and how he had worked with the Resistance in France during the war. The Chief had attempted to find out Morton's war records, but trying to get any information about a secret organisation much less something that had happened 20 odd years ago was nigh on impossible. Although no new information had come to light, he was worried that the powers-that-be might bring in the Mets.

The Chief had said "I have an old friend in a high place I will give him a call."

He went down for a coffee and was talking to Reg when Frank came running down the stairs into the collators.

"Ralph, Ralph we have another murder on our patch, it has all the hallmarks of our man."

"When and where?" Renton looked at his watch. 10.42.

"Discovered at 9.50am at the Lucky Horseshoe Riding Stables near Austerfield, not far from Bawtry."

Renton turned to Reg "Get Doc Wells and either Blot or Peter, and any of the team here today. Show me the way Frank."

5 minutes later with Frank driving they headed for Bawtry.

Renton said "I am sure I have heard the name Austerfield before."

Frank said "Probably when you were at school, Austerfield is the birthplace of William Bradford, the Pilgrim Father who sailed on the Mayflower."

They drove through Bawtry on the A614, through what there was of Austerfield and came to a turning where a constable was pointing them down the road.

"Just down there sir. On the right."

As they arrived at the stables they could see a cottage to the left of the stables and a large paddock to the right.

Frank said "This should be good. The sergeant out the front of the stables is Amos Arkwright, he's a bit Yorkshire."

"A bit what?" Renton said.

"You'll see."

Frank got out of the car and walked to the uniformed sergeant and they shook hands.

The sergeant said "Hey up me old mucker how's tha gettin' on?"

"I'm fine." Frank said "Can I introduce you to Detective Chief Inspector Renton."

Sergeant Amos shook Renton's hand and said "Eee a bloomin' DCI bloomin' grand."

Renton said "Hello sergeant, where is the body?"

"Ovver here." He led him to the fifth stable, the one nearest to the paddock and furthest from the cottage. "There's yon feller. Up to 'is neck in hoss shit."

Renton and Frank looked in the stable. The victim was sitting on the ground in the corner of the stable covered up to his neck in manure.

Frank said "Wilson."

Amos said "Ay, Ernie Wilson here in the not so lucky Horseshoe stable."

"Who found him?" Renton said.

"His lass Marilyn, she's int cottage."

Just then Doctor Wells appeared and also Peter.

Doctor Wells said "In here I presume chaps, hello Amos how are you?" he didn't wait for a reply and went into the stables. He examined the body. "Strangled I think and his mouth is full of manure so may have choked at the same time." He beckoned Renton into the stable and said in a low whisper "This is your killer Ralph but I shall know more later." He turned to Peter and said "All yours young man. The mortuary men should be here in about 20 minutes."

Renton said "Chance of a time of death?

"Oh I think within the last two to three hours." He looked at his watch and said "Maybe a bit more. 7 to 8am."

Frank said to Amos "Peter here is the designated officer for today, so once he has finished the mortuary team will come and take the body away, once they have gone we want this stable locked up and a guard put on it."

Renton and Frank then went to the cottage to see Mrs. Wilson.

Renton said "I forgot most of our team are rest day except for Tina, can you get on the car radio and get her down here."

Frank said. "Already done, she's on her way"

Renton knocked on the door and then walked in and identified himself to the two women at a kitchen table. The one not crying said "I am Freda, Marilyn's sister. As you can see she is quite upset. Can we do this later?"

Renton said "We have a female officer coming. Frank can you go and see the sergeant and get the lowdown on what he knows about this place and Wilson." He then turned to Freda, taking her to one side and said "Did Marilyn find him?"

"Yes. Ernie turns the horses out into the paddock if it's not raining. Every morning at 6am. The third, fourth and fifth stable are for the horses. The first is for storing the feed and the second is his office. No one, not even Marilyn, is allowed in the office. It's his retreat from the world. The stable lad Greg doesn't come in on a Sunday. It's his day off."

Renton said "Is Marilyn married to Ernie?"

"No they are not married but have been living together for years."

"So what time did she find him?"

"Ten to ten. He mucks out the stables and sees that the horses are fed. He then usually does a bit of paperwork and she brings him a sandwich and a cuppa. I heard her scream and ran to the stable and found her in the stable. So I guided her back here and rang Sergeant Arkwright at Bawtry Police Station. We have their telephone number because we had a break in a couple of months ago. We all know Amos and he came straight away."

He was just about to speak when Tina came in. He introduced her to Marilyn and Freda. He went outside and beckoned to Tina to follow. He said "I would like you to stay here today and over the next few days. Come in civvies and get to know Marilyn and help them out. I am told you are into horses."

"Oh yes sir, born on a farm."

"That's great, so get to know them, help out and see what's what. Once Marilyn is more composed then take a statement. I will get Sergeant Arkwright to drop some statement forms in."

He then went back to the stable and saw Peter. "Just finished in the stable sir and the office. Only one set of prints in the office, but two sets on the tack."

"That's probably the stable lad Greg. I can't see the killer messing around with the tack, can you?"

Just then the mortuary team arrived. They went in the stable and 10 minutes later came out with the box.

Renton returned to the cottage and said to Freda "Tina is staying here for today, she is into horses and she will help out if you have a change of clothes. Here is my card if you think of anything that may have happened in the past. If you cannot get hold of me then contact Sergeant Arkwright."

Renton then went with Frank to the office in the stables. On the wall was two framed photographs, one of Wilson with Eddy in a stable holding a horse and another of Wilson in police uniform with Miller. They looked through the cabinets and found a couple of glasses and a bottle of brandy. He and Frank then returned to the police station. Renton then telephoned the Chief at his home and told him what had happened.

24

Not so Lucky Horseshoe

Renton arrived in the collators and made himself a strong coffee and a tea for Frank.

Reg said "I took the liberty of getting everyone here for 12.30."

Sure enough by 12.30 everyone was assembled with a drink and settled down.

Renton said "This morning Ernest 'Tug' Wilson was found dead in a stable he owns called the Lucky Horseshoe Riding Stables just outside Austerfield near Bawtry. According to Doctor Wells he had been strangled somewhere between 7am to 8am. He was sitting on the ground in the corner of the stable up to his neck in horse manure, with some in his mouth. Post mortem tomorrow so we will know more then. Wilson turns the 3 horses out into the paddock at 6am every morning, feeds them and mucks out the stables. Between 9.30am to 10am his partner Marilyn Cooper then brings him a sandwich and a cuppa. She found him this morning at ten to ten. At the moment Tina is there. Peter found nothing that would lead us to the killer."

Frank said "According to Sergeant Arkwright, Wilson retired in 1945 and bought the stables in a dilapidated state and has built it up into a thriving business teaching the gentry's children to ride. Don't forget he is a trained accountant. Tina is into horses and will be at the stables over the next few days helping out and seeing what's what. They have a stable lad Greg Johnson who is away for a few days so we need to see him."

Renton then said "I can tell you all now, that Peter here is now our designated fingerprint officer." There was a round of applause. Renton said "Ink has virtually retired and Blot will be retiring in the New Year. Also Peter types all his reports which means we don't have to put up with that scrawl that Ink and Blot call handwriting."

Frank said "So, Jack, David, Dennis and Steve, usual thing out and about, anywhere you can buy fuel ten-mile radius of Austerfield. Look out for the vehicles and posh houses. Tomorrow we will have extra constables doing house to house between here through Austerfield to Bawtry. You lot will be taking statements if the constables get anything."

Frank said "I asked Tina to come back for 5pm, Amos will drop her off."

By 5pm everyone was assembled in the incident room including Tina and Sergeant Arkwright.

Renton said "Tina? any revelations?"

"Oh yes. They had a visit from cap comforter man on Saturday 31st August. Marilyn said he was dressed in the sort of clothing officers wore when they were off duty. He turned up at 11am driving a red Rover. He said his 11 year old niece wanted riding lessons. Freda took him round the stables and showed him the layout and he asked where the owner was. Wilson was actually in Doncaster picking up feed for the horses. 6-foot-tall, white checked shirt, green jumper with leather patches on the elbows, green corduroy trousers and brown leather brogues. Posh accent. I have taken a statement from both of them."

"Excellent, so tomorrow if you can go to the stables say for 9am and the rest of us will be over there by 10am for the house to house. Let's call it a day."

25

SOE

At 9am the briefing started for the 8 constables who would be doing house to house.

Frank said "Now you all have the descriptions of our man and the 2 vehicles he uses, one a Commer van and the other a red Rover. There will be 2 of you with each one of our team. Just ask the locals if they have seen any strangers in their neighbourhood in the last 3 months. You are covering a wide area and you will be in radio contact with Sergeant Arkwright who is the local beat sergeant. Right off you go and good luck."

As they all left the incident room Renton saw Reg answer his telephone. He went into his office.

"That was Margery. Could you see the Chief after morning prayers?"

Renton said "Time for a coffee."

45 minutes later he was sitting with the Chief. He then told the Chief all about the death of Ernest Wilson.

The Chief said "What I am about to tell you is strictly off the record. Recently my wife and I went to London for a few days for a family gathering. At the gathering was an old friend of mine who, during 1939 to 46, was involved with work where he was the link between the Foreign Office and the Ministry of War. A shadowy figure to say the least. He asked me how our investigation was progressing and I told him that we didn't know very much about Michael Morton's past life during the war and that he was involved with a secret service. He said "I like solving mysteries, I will see what I can do."

"5 days later he sent me this typed letter. As you can see there is no address and no signature but inserted into one of the sentences is his codename from the war."

It read "Michael Morton joined the Royal Marines but during the selection process it was discovered that he was a very capable individual and fluent in several languages. He passed all the tests and so he was asked to join SOE, which he did. After several months of training in which he excelled he was parachuted into France to work with the Resistance in Operation Maurizio guiding downed Allied airmen back to England via Spain and Switzerland. During this time, he was captured by the Gestapo and tortured for several days but thanks to his team leader Captain Bond and his team he was rescued. He returned to Britain where he was debriefed. He later was sent to Holland to establish links with their Resistance under Operation Maurizio. Later he was dropped ahead of the D-Day Landings. At the end of the war when SOE was disbanded he was offered a post in an M service which he declined. The last he was heard of, he was working for an office dedicated to tracking down Nazis. Possibly with an organisation part of the fledgling Israeli Secret Service."

Renton said "Maurizio?"

"Yes, Operation Maurizio never existed. Now I would ask you to destroy this letter. As you can see, Morton is a highly trained killer and obviously not a single scruple in relation to those he deems as the enemy. So after reading this I have decided that from now on we will have an unmarked car circulating manned by 2 armed officers. I would suggest Ted Maynard and Jack Bradley. I have written the authorisation for the carrying and, if necessary, the use of firearms."

"Very good sir."

Renton returned to the collators and made a much needed coffee. He said to Reg and Frank "Now on this piece of paper is something that we need to discreetly tell the others. Then destroy it." He handed it to Frank who read it and passed it to Reg. Reg then took out a pair of scissors and cut it up into very fine pieces.

Frank said "That's interesting. Michaels, team leader in the war was a Captain Bond. Any connection to Thomas 'Tommo' Bond, I wonder?"

Renton said "We three and the Chief are the only people to see that. I will reveal the gist of it to the others. Also the Chief has authorised for Ted and Jack to carry firearms and go out in an unmarked car from now until we get Morton. Debrief at 5pm. Now I am ravenous so off to the Diner, Frank?"

Frank said "Monday will be chicken casserole and bananas and custard for pudding."

5pm arrived and everyone was seated. The constables who had been conducting the house to house had already been thanked and released.

Renton said "Today I received a communication about Michael Morton. In the war he served with SOE, captured by the Gestapo and tortured, escaped and continued to the end of the war working for SOE, D-day and all that. He is extremely dangerous so from now on the Chief has authorised that Ted and Jack will be armed and circulate around Doncaster in an unmarked car. As you know I believe that Morton is living somewhere close but having a car means he could be in Manchester or Sheffield or anywhere. We are still looking for Bond. He must be registered with a doctor so for the moment we are looking at doctor's surgeries. David cover Doncaster. Steve the East Riding and Reg will cover the North Riding."

Just then Tina walked in with a familiar looking brown envelope. She put a poppy on the table with 1914 to 1918 written on it and a note which said "Only you and Tommo left now."

Tina said "They got that letter six days before he was killed and as you can see it is addressed to him personally, so Morton must have delivered it."

The telephone rang. Reg picked up and then put it down. "That was Doctor Wells. One of his boys is dropping in the pm report later and he will see you tomorrow."

Renton said. "Righto I think it is time for a pint."

26

Porky Parker

It was Tuesday 10th September 1963. Renton and Frank had returned from lunch. So far there had been nothing from the enquiries at the doctor's surgeries.

Ted came in and said "One of my tasks as a beat officer is to keep tabs on what is happening at the racecourse. I know the Race Manager Stan Elliott quite well and I asked him if they ever took photographs of the winning jockeys and horses with the punters and if so do they have any in the store. He said that they only ever used one photographer and that it was Porky Parker who has a shop in Doncaster so last week I went to the shop but his assistant said he was out on a wedding in Dewsbury."

"Wait a minute, Porky Parker is who?" said Renton.

"Philip Parker a great photographer. He was an official wartime photographer, was attached to a unit that landed on D-day. Anyway after the war he set up in Doncaster and got the contract to take snaps of racecourse punters with the winners."

"Er, just a minute Ted, where does the name Porky come from?"

"He can eat for England. When the army was in France chasing Jerry back to the Fatherland he could find food no matter where. He also won an eating contest in Buxton. 23 pork pies. So as he expanded he got the name Porkpie which became Porky. He is a lovely bloke and if you ever get married he is your man for the photographs. Anyway he rang me yesterday to go to the shop, which we did today and he came up with this." He produced a photograph, it showed Miller holding up a trophy. On one side was the jockey and on the other side was a large woman, Next to her was a large 6-foot-tall man, in a suit holding a large cigar.

Renton looked at the photograph and said "Mr and Mrs Bond I would say." He looked on the back. It was dated 1954.

Renton said "So was there an address to send the photograph to."

Ted looked at his pocket book. "York."

Ted said "Porky remembered it because he said the big chap tipped him twenty quid.

"Righto so everyone here at 5pm for the debrief."

Everyone as usual was sitting drinks in hand.

Renton said "Here is the official report from Doctor Wells's post mortem on Ernest Wilson but as you know he writes a sort of layman's guide to the death and here it is. Morton finds Wilson in his office, bops him on the nose and then ties him to his chair and gags him just like he did with Miller in the library. Again there is chafing on Wilson's calves as he attempts to stand up and go forward as Morton strangles him. Again downward pressure as he kills him. Wilson had manure in his throat and mouth where Morton made him eat the manure. Once dead he unties him and carries him into the stable where a horse had been. He sits him in the corner and covers shovels manure on him up to the neck. He then departs presumably having left his vehicle some distance away. Now I am told that you have not found any records from doctor's surgeries and clinics."

Just then Tina walked in.

"Marilyn Cooper told me that after Wilson received the letter and the poppy he took all his paperwork and anything to do with his past in the army, apart from his medals and stuff to do with the police and burnt it all near the barn. She said he also produced a pistol from a box he kept in a locker in the kitchen. Here is the box. She thinks he carried the pistol on him or kept it in his office." She gave the box to Renton who opened it and took out a paper. "A Webley pistol, it says an Enfield no.2. What do you think Ted?"

Ted looked at the paperwork and said ".38 calibre that would stop you in your tracks. This was standard issue in the 1930s. Used by officers in the army mainly. I bet he nicked this when he was a copper."

Tina said "He also had a shotgun loaded under the bed, which is still there. I didn't touch it, thought I would leave that to Jack or Ted. I have taken another statement. I went to look at the bonfire but everything has been destroyed. It was at the back of the cottage behind some trees. Also, there is a barn. I had a look inside and at one end of it is a large pile of hay bales with targets fitted to them so I asked Marilyn what that was all about and she said that Wilson and Greg the stable hand did target shooting in there sometimes. She then showed me in the locker there was an air rifle, I left that alone as well."

"So you didn't find the pistol?" Frank said.

"No". Tina said. "I thought it might be in his office."

Renton said. "Righto, if you continue at the stables, Frank and I will be there tomorrow and have a good look in that office. Everyone don't forget your pocket books. Look further afield for the doctor's surgeries."

27

Lee Enfield

The next day Renton and Frank went to the stables, arriving at 10am. As they walked to the cottage Marilyn came out with a young man who she introduced as Greg Johnson. They shook hands and Renton said to Greg "Were you allowed into the office at the stables?"

"Oh yes, all the time."

"Let's go there now and I need you to tell me about this pistol that Ernest had."

Marilyn gave the keys to Greg. They all went to the office and Greg opened it, they went in and Greg went to the drawer of the desk and opened it and said "It's gone, it was in here wrapped in this cloth, he pulled out a yellow duster." He then went through the other drawer and then said "Jesus, the rifle has gone as well."

Renton said "A rifle?"

"Yes." Greg said "It was Ernie's favourite. He brought it back from the war, the first war that is, and the ammo as well. It was here propped up in the corner next to the filing cabinet. The ammo was in the drawer there where the pistol had been."

"Was it a souvenir?" Frank said.

"Yes but we used it for target shooting, I even potted a rabbit with it, not much left of it though."

Renton said "So how much ammo was there for the rifle and the pistol?

"There was about 20 rounds left for the rifle and about 30 rounds for the pistol."

"Did you fire the pistol?"

"No that was Ernie's baby, but he did, he was an excellent shot."

Renton said "I would like you to give a statement to Tina when she gets here saying when you last saw the rifle and pistol." He turned to Marilyn and said "Are all the firearms in Ernest's name?"

She said "Yes."

"Then we will take them with us, we will give you a receipt for them. One of our firearm officers will be here soon and could you show him the shotgun under the bed. That will have to come as well."

"Oh thank you." She said "I hate all those things."

Tina arrived with Ted and Jack, and Renton then told her about the target shooting and the Lee Enfield and to get a statement from Greg.

Ted and Jack came out of the cottage. Ted said. "The shotgun was double barrelled, both barrels had these in ready to go." He produced two shells. Jack then said "and these were in the kitchen cupboard." He had a box of 20 shells. He was also carrying a .22 air rifle. They loaded them into the car and left.

At the 5pm briefing Renton told them about the various weapons that Wilson had kept and the fact that Morton had taken the Webley pistol and the Lee Enfield rifle and the ammo for both.

There had been no joy with the various doctor's surgeries. They had also tried the electoral roll for Doncaster and found Miller but not Bond.

28

Happy Birthday

Renton arrived at his desk as usual at 8.30am. He looked at the calendar on his desk. 15th November 1963. What was he going to do for his birthday? His aunt had offered to take him out for dinner to the Danum for dinner. It was over 3 months since the murder of Leonard Miller. Steve, David and Tina were back on CID. Dennis was back on patrol covering Jack's beat as he was still doing the firearms car with Ted. As Reg had said, someone as large as life as Bond would surely have been found. The Chief had been great about it saying that he was sure something would turn up.

Renton's telephone rang making him jump. Instinctively he looked at his watch. 9.15am. He answered in his usual manner and the voice at the other end said "Happy Birthday Ralph." It was Doctor Wells. "What would you like for your birthday?"

Renton said "Michael Morton giving himself up with a full confession."

"Well I cannot give you that but how about me having signed the death certificate not 20 minutes ago for a Thomas Bond born in 1890 in India, will that do? I am at the mortuary awaiting his body."

Renton said "Grisly death? Shot? Stabbed? Had his head cut off?"

"No, looks very mundane, I would say a heart attack."

Renton said "I will be with you very soon." He picked up the photograph of Bond at the races.

20 minutes later he was standing with Doctor Wells looking at Bond. He showed the doctor the photograph.

The mortuary assistant had taken off Bond's pyjamas.

Doctor Wells said "Apart from his face they could be two different people. You say the photograph was taken in 1954 and here he is nine years later. In the photograph is a large man and here we have an emaciated man. The post mortem will tell us what happened but I reckon he has been starved. Unless he has something like cancer."

Renton said "How did you get the job of certifying death?"

"Bond's accountant is a very attractive woman called Jennifer Steel, who I have known for a number of years, professionally of course. I served in the war with her father, a surgeon turned accountant. She telephoned me. I think Bond was sufficiently rich to go private so was not registered with a GP. Jennifer is an intelligent articulate woman and you can explain to her about Bond and his cronies."

"Righto thanks, for that I shall. I'll see the Chief and brief the troops."

"You will need this, her address and telephone number at Bond's house." He scribbled on a piece of notepaper and handed it to Renton.

Back at the station he briefly saw Reg and told him to gather the troops, he made a coffee and then when prayers had finished he went in and told the Chief about Bond. He returned to the incident room and found everyone gathered as usual, drinks in hand.

Reg said "Now that it looks as if we are moving towards a conclusion do not forget the kitty." He rattled the tin. Renton put in a pound note followed by Frank, also a pound note.

Renton said "This morning Doctor Wells wrote out the death certificate for Thomas Bond at the moment looking like a heart attack. So Steve I want you and the rest to start doing house to house around this address. Frank says that it backs onto the racecourse. We want information on the vehicles and the description of Morton. Frank and I will be at the house. Ted and Jack follow us to the house."

Renton rang Miss Steel and asked if he could come and see her."

She said "Yes of course. Doctor Wells said you would ring."

He put down the receiver and said to Frank "Sounds a bit posh."

Frank said "How did Bond look on the slab?"

"Not so grand without his pyjamas on."

29

Thomas Bond

Frank drove Renton to the house which was in the Rosehill area near the racecourse. Ted and Jack followed behind in the unmarked car It was a large imposing house set back from the road, with trees along the wall which partly obscured it from the road. To the left of the house was an ornate shed. From the gateway to the house it was about 40 feet and the drive went past the house along to a detached garage. At the back was quite a small lawned garden and then all along the back wall was various trees and shrubs obscuring the view of the ground that went up to the racecourse. Frank parked the car and said "Why didn't we check this area near the racecourse knowing that Bond and his cronies were mad about the gee-gees."

As they got out of the car the front door opened to show a smartly dressed woman in her mid forties.

"Hello, you must be Ralph Renton." She shook his hand. He noticed she had a firm grip. "I am Jennifer Steel but call me Jenny and you are?" she shook Frank's hand as he said "DS Frank Dipper." Renton then said "These two officers are our firearms officers Ted Maynard and Jack Bradley. While we are talking do you mind if they search the shed and the garage?"

"No not at all." She reached into the hall and produced some keys which she threw to Ted "They will open the shed and the summerhouse and the garage."

She then showed Renton and Frank into the house. She turned to a young woman inside. "Mary could you do a flask of coffee and a pot of tea with cups and cake for four, and bring it into the lounge in 15 minutes, thank you." She then showed them into the lounge.

Both Renton and Frank looked around and then looked at each other, it reeked of money. An oil painting on the wall that had to be Bond's father, antique furniture, a tiger skin rug in front of the fireplace and various artefacts from India.

As they sat down she said "Yes, I know what you are thinking, a bit too much. Thomas was born in India where his father was very high up in the Colonial Service and various Maharajahs liked to say thank you for all the little jobs he sorted out for them."

Renton said "Do you know the name Michael Morton?"

"Doctor Wells is a family friend, he and dad served together in the war. I don't know anybody by the name Michael Morton but the description Dr Wells gave me matches exactly with the person I know as Robert Bond Junior, Thomas's nephew."

"Where is Robert Bond at the moment?"

"He has an import export business and on Wednesday he was flying out to Germany on one of his many trips."

"Can you tell us about Thomas Bond?"

"Thomas Bond and his brother Robert senior were both born in Dalousie in India. Their father worked in the Colonial Service as I said before but he was an extremely wealthy man and both sons had the finest education. When their father died Robert took over the business and increased their wealth. In 1908 Thomas entered the military, went to Sandhurst, was commissioned and went into the Royal Engineers. When war broke out he was posted to France and early on was wounded and on recovery, which was about the end of 1914, he was posted to Etaples where he stayed for the whole of the war. At the end of the war he declined promotion and joined the Metropolitan Police. He was bisexual and during his time in the war and in the police his lover was Leonard Miller, who I know has been murdered."

"So why did he get married?"

"Because of his contacts he knew he would need to be married to advance his career so he met and married Winifred Dobson. She was from quite a wealthy family but her brother who had inherited the lot, blew it on various schemes and wine, women and song. He then blew his brains out leaving Winifred destitute. Thomas had known the family so they married. She got regular sex and the good life, champagne, good food and cigars and Thomas got respectability. By this time he was fabulously wealthy, his brother Robert had sold their ocean going ships, but still had shares in that company. They were bringing all the things that the wealthy craved, spices, silks and opium and all this stuff." She pointed to the furniture and the artefacts. "Robert very early on had latched on to the fact that there were various minerals to be mined in South America and Africa. He had a large house in Rio and ran operations from there. He split everything 50/50 with Thomas. When Robert senior died he left his property and money to Thomas."

"So where do you fit in with all this?"

"Steel Associates was started by my father after the second war. He had seen enough blood as a surgeon in 1939 to 45 so trained as an accountant. Our main office is in York and I started running the business in there but opened a branch here in Doncaster. My office is actually in the study next door. We have mainly 8 very wealthy clients and Thomas is one." She then went out of the room and said to Mary "Let's have the drinks in the conservatory."

There was a knock on the door and she let in Ted and Jack. She went in the lounge and said to Renton and Frank "Let's go into the conservatory with your chaps."

Thomas Bond Part 2

"Shall I be mother?" said Jenny as she poured the tea and coffee, "Tuck into the cake you chaps."

Renton, after a bite of Victoria sponge and a sip of coffee, said "So why did Bond buy such a big house?"

"Originally he bought an old farmhouse on the outskirts of York with a barn. He then contacted Steel Associates to handle his money, stocks and shares. That was in 1948, my father then handled his accounts. The idea was that he could then entertain his friends and they could enjoy York races but he was looking for a house with a large cellar which this house has. He has an extensive wine collection with a lot of vintage champagne worth a lot of money so he bought this house, again lots of bedrooms for his pals so they could go to the races."

"So what year did he buy this one?"

"Winifred died in 1955 and he then decided that he needed somewhere secure for the wine and champers so bought this house in 1956. He became a little paranoid about security and he cut the ties to his chums except for Leonard, I think that is why he moved here. I was working from my flat in Doncaster and he suggested I move in here, all very above board. Dad had died, also in 1955, so it sort of made sense. Also I would escort him to functions within the Metropolitan Police and the Lodge and having his financial assets in the house was good for him. Very early on in 1960 he had a massive stroke, he couldn't move and could just about speak. He asked me to telephone this chap in London and just say that he had had a stroke. It was all very mysterious and within 2 weeks his nephew Robert turned up."

Renton said "Do you still have that number?"

She went into the study and then came out with a piece of notepaper and handed it to Renton.

"I will have this checked out and see who it is. Please carry on."

"Well, we needed someone to look after him, this was immediately after the stroke. Thomas point blank refused to use the NHS, he had always used a private doctor from Harley Street. I dread to think of the cost, well I know what it cost. Anyway, this man came to see him and gave him a prescription and said the best thing he could do was lose weight and lay off·the rich food and alcohol, especially the brandy and cigars. Of course he completely refused to do that so we had a chef come in and Mary, who is actually a nurse. Shortly after the doctor had been, Robert turned up and introduced himself. He produced a passport to show who he was. I asked him some questions about Thomas and he passed muster and has been here ever since. He nursed Thomas and would read out his stocks and shares in the Financial Times. At first he would take him out in the car but as time went on it was just too much for Thomas and that stopped about 18 months ago. It's a blessing in disguise that he has been here because it means that Mary can be part-time."

"Can you describe the person you know as Robert Bond or have a photograph?"

"No photo." She then described him a dead ringer for Morton.

"Do you know when he is coming back?"

"He said just before Christmas."

"Does he have an address in London that you know about?"

"I do have a telephone number in London that I have rung before to pass on messages for Thomas." She scribbled the number on the piece of paper and handed it to him. "The telephone was usually answered by a young woman with an accent, rough guess I would say Spanish."

Renton said "If he caused Bond to have that heart attack that is the last you will see of him. He has been seen driving a red Rover, do you know whose that is?"

"Thomas bought that for himself just before he had the stroke."

"Could you show me the bedroom Morton used?"

She took them upstairs and into his bedroom which was quite large. Double bed, a desk and chair and a wardrobe. Renton opened the wardrobe and said "Well, well." Inside was a blazer and the clothes he had worn when he went to the riding stables, also a couple of shirts and a regimental tie. They went downstairs.

Renton said "We don't have any fingerprints for Michael Morton so I would like our fingerprint detective to come and take elimination prints from you and Mary. He will go to the mortuary to get the necessary prints there. If you can show him where Morton would have been and what he touched that would be very helpful. The fingerprint detective is called Peter Johns. I will get him this afternoon. Is that okay with you?

"Of course, I will be here for the rest of the day."

Outside Renton said to Ted "Whatever you found in the garage and shed, let's talk about it when we get back to the incident room."

30

Spotless

Back in the incident room, Ted made them all a drink and then they sat in the incident room where they were joined by Reg. Renton rang Peter Johns and gave him the address and asked him to look for fingerprints.

"So Ted, I could see you itching to tell me what you found when we were in the house" said Renton.

Ted said "I did the shed, there is a mower and tools and some jars of weed killer. The summerhouse has a view of the race course and there is an armchair and a table with a bottle of brandy and some glasses covered in dust. I reckon with all the doors and windows open you could hear the loudspeakers announcing the races and the results. But it's what Jack found."

Jack said "The Commer van is in the garage, it's spotlessly clean inside but we should let Peter loose in there. In the garage there is a locker with two sets of black overalls, boots and a certain cap comforter. Some false plates and a commando knife, very sharp. There is a small room upstairs with a window that looks down the drive to the house but wrapped up in a towel is a Lee Enfield rifle and a several clips of ammo for it. Also some ammo for the Webley pistol which is not there. Also a box of about 30 rounds, I wasn't too sure but I guessed for a Colt automatic. Ted had a look at it and he confirmed it's for a Colt automatic, the sort the Yanks had in the war. However I couldn't find the Colt."

"I will just ring Jenny and get her to tell Peter to do the sheds and the garage." Renton said.

Behind his back Jack pouted and mouthed 'Jenny'.

Renton came back and said "He has allegedly gone to Germany, he has no more to kill on his dad's list and the Rover has not been spotted by anybody so I reckon he has a bolthole somewhere for the car and himself and it has to be in London." He turned to Reg "Here are a couple of numbers Jenny gave me can you check them out they are both in London. See if our pals in the Met can help. 5pm debrief. I shall now go and see the Chief.

Debrief. Everyone was present. Renton relayed the conversation with Jenny as well as the clothes Jack had found in the bedroom that matched the description of the cap comforter man. He then said about the garage and the weapons and also that Michael Morton had the Webley and a Colt with him. He then recapped on the description from Father Dominic of the Pig man, and from Marilyn Cooper at the stables.

He said "So he comes to Doncaster and uses this address to go out and kill Bond's cronies. I saw Bond's body at the mortuary and he is emaciated almost like he has been starved, not the Bond we have seen in photographs so is that part of his revenge? Once I see the post mortem report we will know. So you lot what have you got?"

David said "Not a lot. You cannot see the house from the road, you have to go to the drive to get a view of it. One elderly lady said that she thought she had seen a delivery van there, black in colour. She couldn't say when. That pretty much says it for all the residents, it seems they keep themselves to themselves and the fact that Bond's house has trees covering it from the front doesn't help.

Just then Peter came in, it had been a long day.

Renton said "Tell me you have a fingerprint of Michael Morton."

"Nothing, he is a very careful man and they have a cleaner that is on a par with Mrs. Jenkins for efficiency. I have just come from the mortuary and Doc Wells said he would have the report for you tomorrow. I did the garage and that is spotless."

"Tomorrow, Steve and I will go to the house and take a statement from Jenny about Morton turning up and all that. I will be in the Red Lion at 6pm and the wallet will be open for 10 minutes only."

31

Parkin the Cake

Renton arrived at the station at his usual time, made a coffee and then went through all the statements they had taken so far. He was joined by Frank and then Steve who both made themselves a drink.

He said to Reg "Have you had anything back from Scotland Yard about those two telephone numbers from Jenny?"

"I did get a very brief call yesterday from a DS Jackson who should be ringing sometime this morning."

One hour later Renton and Steve were with Jenny in the kitchen she had shared with Thomas Bond and Michael Morton, the man she knew as Robert Bond, she served them a coffee each.

"No Mary today then Jenny?" said Renton

"No I have given her the weekend off."

"We need to take a statement from you, really from when Morton arrived here. Do you keep a diary that would show his movements so we can compare them with the dates of the murders?"

"I am an accountant remember so I have a business diary and a separate diary for the house, which is mainly him coming and going and expenses for shopping, the car service and medicines for Thomas."

Jenny went into the study and produced the diary and then Renton showed her the dates of the murders.

"Righto the first murder was on Sunday 5th November 1961, that was Webb in Liverpool."

Jenny said "Yes, he went to Germany leaving here on the 1st of November and came back on the 15th of November."

"Next one was MacCrae on Sunday, 3rd February this year 1963."

"Let me see. He went to Spain on 27th of January and came back on the 17th February."

"Next one is Miller, he was killed on Saturday 3rd August this year."

"Yes, here we are, he said South America from 28th July to 22nd August. He made a big thing about this trip because he said he was going back to the house his father had left for him in his will."

"That's strange because Matthew Armstrong the preacher was of the opinion that he sold the house in Dulwich and the shop. Last of all we have Wilson another Sunday 8th September this year."

"Went to Germany on 1st of September and came back on 15th September."

"That's excellent so Steve will write your statement and include all this in it. I shall go for a stroll, I will get the keys and look at the outbuildings and the garage. See you in a bit."

Renton went and looked in the shed. Nothing unusual. 3 jars marked weed killer. Next he went into the summerhouse at the end of the garden and sat in the armchair. Then looked through the cabinet, newspaper cuttings from the Daily Express about what the police were doing in London. Then he went into the garage. Just as Peter had said it was all very clean, even the Commer was spotless. He went back to the garden and sat on an old chair. He thought what if Morton had done a runner and wasn't going to come back. Perhaps he could make Morton think that Bond had left him a lot of money in his will to lure him back. Morton knew that Bond was loaded, he would talk it over with Jenny and then with the Chief. He went back into the garage and went upstairs and imagined Morton pulling up in the car. Have him dead to rights in what could be a cross fire. Jack here with the Lee Enfield which looked in working order. Himself out the front door pistol pointing at Morton. Someone upstairs say Ted looking down from a bedroom, window maybe another gun from behind the shed.

"Ralph, wake up. It's coffee and cake time." It was Jenny shouting from the back door. "You were in your own thoughts just then." She said.

"I have had a look at the various buildings and there is nothing that shows what Morton actually does with this import and export business. Did he ever bring stuff back or paperwork to show for it?"

Jenny said "He had a briefcase and occasionally pulled out paperwork but I never pried. I have enough of my own."

He got up and joined her and Steve in the kitchen. She said "here is some parkin cake, I only bake this when we are getting into winter."

Renton and Steve helped themselves to a generous slice each.

Renton said to Jenny "Does Morton have money in his own right?"

"Well the real Robert Bond didn't get a penny from his father, they were two peas in a pod and constantly arguing according to Thomas. He left everything to Thomas. Now as Michael Morton I couldn't say. Maybe this import export business is a real thing, who knows. Thomas paid him two hundred pounds a month for expenses and he could ask for money for petrol, maintenance."

"Does he stand to get anything from Thomas?

"£125,000, some stocks and shares and he can have the car. But of course if he is really Morton he won't get a penny or anything else."

"What if we used that "inheritance" to lure him back here and then arrest him."

"Well, there would have to be a will reading and if we stick with protocol an obituary, then funeral then a will reading."

Renton said "We know that Thomas died of a heart attack either naturally or caused by Morton. If we let his arrogance make him believe that we poor souls believe he died of a heart attack, then the obituary, funeral and will reading will seem just the norm. Would you be prepared to go through with all that?"

"Yes, but what if Morton somehow gave Thomas some sort of drug to cause that heart attack, wouldn't you have to keep the body until the trial?"

"No, if Doctor Wells can prove that Morton killed Thomas using some sort of a drug then with the permission of the Attorney General we could go ahead with the obituary and the rest."

Just then the telephone in the hall rang, Jenny put her finger to her lips and answered it. "It's for you Ralph."

Renton listened then put the receiver. "Doctor Wells is coming in at 3pm to give us the news on the post mortem and the Chief wants to see me at 1pm."

Forty minutes later they were back at the station.

32

Doctor Wells

Back at the station Renton and Steve went down to the incident room. Steve added Jenny's witness statement to the file.

Renton said to Reg "Did you get a reply from DS Jackson in London?"

"Yes, the telephone number that Thomas Bond asked Jenny to ring belongs to MI6 and the other telephone to this Spanish woman or whatever she is, it's an address in Streatham. He says for you to ring today or tomorrow, the address is a flat one of six in a block sandwiched between 2 shops. The shop directly next to the flat has been closed for years."

Renton said "MI6? The mystery deepens. What does the Chief want of me?"

"He was twittering on about having an armed presence in the house to protect the fair damsel called Jenny."

"Bit dramatic and what of the Doc?"

"Said Bond definitely died of a heart attack but of something other than a natural cause."

"Righto, I shall sort out my diary and grab a sandwich and then see the Chief."

Right on 1pm Renton walked into the Chief's office.

"Hello Ralph good of you to come, I know you are very busy, now what about an armed presence in the house in case Morton turns up, thinking of Miss Steel."

"Well she is no threat to Morton, Thomas Bond has left quite a bit of money in his will to Robert Bond but has he the guts to turn up and claim it, him being Michael Morton. The only way he can get the money is through a will reading."

"I see. I haven't informed the Home Office about Ted and Jack carrying because they will then try and force the Mets on us. However I am on very good terms with the Chief Officer at the City of Sheffield, we were at Cambridge together. He has a couple of lads, ex RMP, and prepared to lend them to us if we need a bit of extra firepower. Keep it in Yorkshire. What do you think?"

"Very good sir."

"Yes I thought so, our boys doing the day shift and the Redcaps doing the night duty."

Renton returned to the incident room and then told Frank about his thoughts on luring Morton back.

Frank said "If we get the Chief on board then I am sure he will convince the Attorney General and the Home Office round to his way of thinking."

"Righto let's get everyone in ready for the typhoon that is Doctor Wells."

Right on 3pm in walked the Doctor.

"Hello chaps and lady, waiting for me?"

Reg said "Would you like a drink Doctor?"

"Oh gosh no, too early for a gin and tonic what."

He handed the report to Renton and said "That's the formal bit out of the way. Now Miss Steel said that when Bond had his first stroke he was a large corpulent man of 69 years with a fondness of good food, champagne for breakfast every day of his adult life, brandy and cigars. His idea of exercise was handing out large wads of cash on the gee-gees. So along came the stroke and despite what his personal doctor told him he continued with the champers and the rest of it. At this point his nephew comes along and takes over his diet allegedly. I say that because here we are 4 years later and he has had another stroke and the person lying in the mortuary is, to say the least, malnourished. He was also given sleeping tablets on a regular basis probably to keep him quiet. You wouldn't taste it in a glass of champagne but there was something else in his blood stream which I have sent to London to a colleague for his analysis. It could be some sort of a poison possibly bringing on that heart attack. I have examined his body and near his left ankle are several punctures from a syringe so look out for a syringe hidden somewhere on the property."

Ted said "In the shed were several jars all marked weed killer two with black writing and one in red."

"Very good. Seal them and bring them to the mortuary and I will pass them to a chemist friend and let him run some tests to see what they are. "

Renton said "When can we bury him?"

"Not until we know what that substance in his bloodstream is, my colleague will telephone me the result then you can put him in the ground and he will post an official document for your murder file. So if that is it I shall be off." He looked around and then left.

Renton then said "I have spoken with Jenny about luring Morton back here so we can arrest him. The fact that he spoke to Marilyn Cooper and her sister as well as the identical clothes in the wardrobe at the house is enough to haul him in. Also we need to find this syringe. It may be in the car he is using but I think we need to have a good look around the house, garage and outhouses. So tomorrow Frank, Ted, Jack, Steve and I will get to the house for 10am and I will sort out with her a plan to get him back. I will ring her now and then give DS Jackson a call."

Steve said "If we have 4 people who have seen him and spoken to him couldn't we have an identification parade. Father Dom saw him just before Miller's murder and the two sisters were all at the murder scene at the stables."

Renton said "Yes we could do that."

Renton rang Jenny and explained what they hoped to do. She said "I will have bacon rolls ready to keep your men sustained."

He then rang DS Jackson. apologising for the lateness of the call.

DS Jackson. "That's ok boss, that's what we get paid for. The MI6 number is very interesting and my DI has clearance to ask them what it's all about because why would your killer have that number? He is on the blower now to them so I will call you in about an hour hopefully. Your collator filled me in on your suspect and the fact that his surname is Morton could be a coincidence. The telephone goes down to a flat which is one of six. It is next to the old shop which originally was one of 3 owned by a Horace Morton. Unfortunately, two of the shops were destroyed by a bomb in the war. So after your collator called I got the local bobby to go to the flats on a bogus call and the young woman who answered the door said her name was Deborah Smith. I called up the investigator at the Royal Mail sorting office for that area. They keep a sort of index and the mail going to that flat has the name Deborah Morton. Our contact in the Foreign office come passport office says that a Susanna Ortega gave that address when she entered the country. Our bobby said she had an accent. Oh, lookout here is the DI."

There was a pause while the phone was handed over.

"Hello DCI Renton, I am DI Randall Special Branch. We were very interested when your man gave us that number. It goes straight to their index office. Basically their personnel files. It would seem that Thomas Bond was given that number by his nephew Robert Bond as a next of kin. Bond junior was originally in SOE during the war and on his team was a Mike Morton, they were quite pally. When the war ended SOE was disbanded and its men were given the option of joining an M organisation. Bond's team were trained killers basically but picked for their speciality in languages and being smart able to think on their feet so to speak."

Renton said "We don't have a photograph of Morton or Bond or their fingerprints. Not that the killer left any, in fact no forensic evidence at all."

"I cannot help you with the mugshots or prints. We are putting a surveillance team on that address in Streatham, if any man turns up fitting the description we have or in a Rover he will be nicked and on his way to you. Here is Jacko he has something to say."

There was crackle as DI Jackson took the phone.

"Hello boss, I will be running the team. By the way that old shop next door is all closed up curtains pulled and the Royal Mail say that it has not had any post since the early fifties but it is owned by a company called Impact Clothiers, which I think is maybe a front for something else. Now if you are planning to nick Morton or Bond we will have a warrant ready to do the flat and the old shop because I think they are linked, just a gut feeling though."

"Thank you DS Jackson I will keep you up to date on what we are doing."

Renton then made another telephone call and then returned to the collators. Everyone had gone home except for Frank and Reg. Renton made a black coffee and then told them about the conversation with DS Jackson and DI Randall.

He then said "Now Reg, tomorrow is a Sunday and you can take the day off if you wish."

Reg said. "No fear. Mrs P has her WI cronies coming for a roast. Sod that."

33

A Kings Ransom

Renton arrived at 9am and looked at his calendar. Sunday 17th November 1963, the 106th day of the murder investigation and they didn't really have any forensic proof on Morton. No doubt they could tie him into certain things with ID parades with Father Dominic and the Pig man and Marilyn Cooper but not a lot else. He needed to find that syringe and hope it had something in it that was the same as what was in Bond's bloodstream. Frank had stood down David and Tina from the investigation.

He went down to the collators, only Reg was there, he made them a drink. "How did you get on with that telephone call." He winked.

Renton said "It was to a friend I worked with in the war in the Intelligence Corps. He now works for a department allied to the Ministry of Defence, I don't ask too many questions. I asked him if he could find a photograph of Michael Morton and Robert Bond with roughly the same year of birth give or take a year or so if he can he will post it to me. We can see which one has been living at the house. I know they will be 25 year old photographs but we will see what Jenny thinks."

Just then Frank and Austin walked in. Austin said "Buttered scones for later." Reg put them in a drawer.

Frank said "I counted them and if you have one there will be 7 left."

Reg just smiled.

Frank said to Renton "I have the car keys and Ted and Jack have just left for Jenny Steele's house."

As they walked up to the front door it opened and Jenny said "The kettle is on and Ted and Jack are already into a bacon roll each."

Frank said "You Royal Marines show no respect for senior ranks."

Renton and Frank polished off a roll each, had a drink and then Renton said to Jenny "While these fine chaps are looking for the poison and syringe we need a plan for the dates of obituary, funeral and will reading. Let's presume that the result is poison and we get it tomorrow so we then need a date for the obituary."

Jenny said "Before that, let me show you something."

She opened a door in the kitchen, showing a toilet. To the left of the toilet she opened another door to reveal a spiral staircase. She switched on a light and then went down the spiral staircase,with Renton and Frank behind her. At the bottom she unlocked another door, turned on another light and went through the door followed by Renton and Frank who noticed a sort of clamminess. Renton and Frank stood there gobsmacked. There was row after row of wine bottles.

Jenny said "One hundred and twenty three bottles of vintage claret. Fifty-seven bottles of the finest cognac and one hundred and thirty-two bottles of champagne of which nineteen currently would fetch a thousand pound each at auction. A lot of this was purloined by Thomas and his cronies in the war. It was shipped to his brother in London. The nineteen bottle of champers were purchased in dribs and drabs."

Renton said "It's a King's Ransom."

Jenny said "A lot of weaponry disappeared, guess who was looking after the books?"

"Miller." said Renton.

Yes, and it went to the brother who then sold it on. Tinpot regimes in South America and the Spanish Civil War took a lot. If you walk through the cellar there is a door at the back that goes into a tunnel which leads to another door which goes into the inspection pit in the garage. Originally all this was stored in the barn in York, but Thomas wanted somewhere more secure so he paid some man to find the right place and he found this house. This lot was delivered into the garage and then Miller, Webb and Bond moved it into the cellar. As you can see there is a table and four chairs where Thomas and his pals would work their way through various bottles."

"Does Morton know all about this, what's down here?"

"He knows that Thomas has a lot of alcohol stored down here, he knows about the tunnel from the inspection pit but the tunnel is like a room so he just thinks it is for storage. There is a rack of several bottles of rum, whisky and brandy. The keys from the house to the room near the pit are all kept in my handbag but he would have the key to that door attached to the garage keys."

"That is it." said Renton. "I bet that is where the syringe is. In the pit or that room."

Jenny said "Let's go and look."

They went back up into the house and went outside to find Ted putting something in the boot. Ted said "I have sealed the three jars and put them in the boot."

"Righto, back to the garage we have something to show you."

They all went inside the garage. Renton said to Jack to release the handbrake and move the van forwards.

He did so and then Renton climbed into the pit and found the light. Jenny handed him a key and said "It is towards the garage door."

Renton found the lock and then crouching down he went down some steps into what looked like a room. He straightened up. He could see the racks of alcohol, Jenny shouted down "The other door looks like a book rack."

He looked at the rack and right in the corner on the floor was a small leather satchel. He pulled a pair of gloves out his pocket, put them on and carefully picked the satchel up and went back into the light. He handed it up to Frank. Renton then went back up the stairs into the garage. He opened the satchel on the work bench and pulled out a cigar box tied with ribbon. He undid the ribbon, opened the box and quietly said "Eureka."

Inside the box resting on cotton wool was two syringes and a small bottle.

Frank said "Look. One of the syringes has still got some liquid inside."

Renton closed the box tied it up and put it in the satchel very carefully.

He said "Ted, take this to Peter Johns to look for any prints. Explain to Peter not to get any fluid on his hands then tomorrow, the satchel and those jars go to the mortuary."

With that Ted and Jack returned to the police station, Renton and Frank locked up the garage and then returned with Jenny to the kitchen.

As they had a drink Renton said "I think we will wait for the result from the doc's friend and then plan the obituary and all that, later. Jenny would you like to come with Frank and I to the Red Lion for a roast dinner?"

She said "I will lock up and get my coat."

Renton and Frank returned Jenny to the house after lunch and then discussed the obituary and the rest of the plan.

Renton said "Let's say the fluid is poison so what day can we have the funeral?"

Jenny opened her diary "I know the local funeral director because he organised dad's funeral. You have to give good notice in the obituary for the funeral date. So if today is Monday the 18th November and the funeral was on Wednesday 4th December, that's 17 days from now, so have the obituary come out on the week before that is the 27th November, again a Wednesday."

Renton wrote down the dates and then said "And the reading of the will?"

"Say 2 weeks after the funeral on 18th December." Said Jenny.

"That's great" said Frank. "After interviewing and charging him, he could go to York and then Liverpool and then be in prison for Christmas."

Jenny said "Have they got enough evidence to charge him?"

Renton said "Not really, not forensic yet. It depends on what is in the syringe. If that is positive then we can charge him with Bond's murder, he will know that he is looking at life in prison. As for Miller and Wilson's murders we could have the identification parade. What we really need is a witness who saw him on that morning that he killed Miller. By the time he has appeared at the Old Bailey they will have got rid of capital punishment. He might decide to confess, who knows. Well we had better be getting back to the station and tomorrow I will see the Chief with these dates and hopefully by then Doc Wells will have a result."

Back at the station, everyone was coming in for the debrief. Ted, Jack, Steve, Austin and Reg were there as Renton and Frank came in. Frank made Renton and himself a drink.

Renton said "We are waiting for a result from Doc Wells about whether it was poison or not, we then go ahead with the obituary and funeral and then the reading of the will to hopefully lure Morton back. Tomorrow I will see the Chief and give him the details of all that."

Peter came into the room and said "Can I add something?"

"Yes of course." Renton said.

"I have found a print on the bottle and syringe that was in the cigar box."

Peter continued "It looks like maybe a thumb print on the bottle and a finger print on the syringe."

"Well done Peter." Renton said. "We need those prints to be taken to the fingerprint bureau at Scotland Yard, a job for Ted tomorrow."

Ted nodded.

Just then in breezed Doctor Well. "Hello chaps, I have just received a telephone call from my man in London and the fluid in Bond's bloodstream is a poison, aconite. Highly poisonous. Otherwise known as Monkshood or wolf's bane. I am sure that it is the same liquid in the syringe but we will see what my chemist friend says. So my man in London will send me a formal report which I shall pass on to you and the chemist will do the same."

Renton said "That's from a plant. How would Morton convert the plant into the liquid?"

"Boiling it I would think. He then injected into the lower leg to allow for it to take say 24 hours or so to get to his heart and then wallop, the heart attack. Well, must fly."

Renton said "Righto, let's call it a day. Ted first thing tomorrow up to London, I will ring them tomorrow at 9am and warn them of your impending arrival. All we need is Morton's fingerprints when we arrest him."

34

Henry Sykes

Renton arrived at his office, it was 9am. He telephoned Scotland Yard and asked to be put through to the fingerprint bureau and told them about the prints that were on their way and who was bringing them. He then turned his attention to the files which had appeared in his tray. The note attached was from DI Johnny Martin so he knew they would be in order. He had a quick look through and then signed them up. He knew that Johnny would not put his name to anything that wasn't correct. He telephoned Margery and asked if he could see the Chief after morning prayers so she booked him in for 10.30am. He checked his post slot and there was a brown envelope addressed to him. Back at his desk he opened the envelope. It contained two photographs and a brief note saying "Please destroy, taken prior to entry into SOE. Morton for Royal Marines and Bond to Grenadier Guards". It was signed 'Ajax'. Renton thought 'after all these years he still uses his codename from the war.' Better safe than sorry.

One photograph was of Michael Morton aged 20 years and the other was of Robert Bond also aged 20 years. What was amazing was that they could be brothers. He went down to the incident room made a coffee and then said to Frank. "Have a look at this?"He gave him the photograph of Morton.

Frank turned it over "A young Michael Morton, that building behind is the officer's mess in Wellington Barracks."

Renton then gave him the photo of Bond

Frank said "A brother?" turned it over and said "Bugger me it's Bond. They could be brothers. From a secret contact I presume."

"Yes for our eyes only."

The telephone in the collators rang. Reg answered and said "Yes I will tell him."

Reg said "Why don't you go to morning prayers and bring them up to date on the murders."

"Wonderful," Renton said. He pocketed the two photographs and wrote himself a memo. At 9.30 he was sat in the Chief's office with Johnny Martin, DS Moran, Chief Inspector Fox and a man in a 3 piece suit.

The Chief said "Ralph I would like to introduce you to Henry Sykes." They shook hands and he said "Hello DCI Renton, we meet at last." Renton noticed the firm grip. They sat down. The Chief continued "Henry is here on behalf of Walter from the Joint Committee, who has wrenched his ankle due to slipping on his kitchen floor. Could you bring us up to date with the murder investigation."

Renton then briefly set out the committing of the Yorkshire murders and then what had happened so far and about the breakthrough of the syringes and the poison. He then outlined what was going to happen with the obituary, funeral and reading of the will. When he had finished the Chief said "I will relieve you from the rest of prayers but at the end could you show Henry round the incident room and some of the exhibits?"

"Yes of course sir."

Renton left and then returned to the collators and told Reg and Frank what was going to happen.

"Another strong coffee I think. He then laid out the exhibits and the file. Saying to Reg "Don't cover up the photographs let's see if he has the stomach for them."

One hour later the Chief brought down Mr Sykes, he introduced him to Reg and said to Renton "A word Ralph." He went into the corridor and said to Renton "Unlike our good friend Walter, Henry will be the epitome of discretion, he can be trusted with the details. Ex RN Captain." With that the chief went back to his office.

Renton said "Would you like a drink Henry?"

"Why yes. Strong black coffee, no sugar. Thank you."

Renton then told him about the murders in York and Liverpool and the way they were killed and then the photographs of the dead men. He didn't turn a hair. Renton then showed him the exhibit from Miller's death and the photographs of the exhibits from York and Liverpool. They then sat down in the collators.

Henry said "Do you think that the killer will turn up for the will reading. He must know that you know how Bond died?"

"I am banking his arrogance is such that he thinks we are incompetent and won't trace the aconite. He injected a very small dose and Bond was in a very weak state. Also he thinks that Jenny Steel has been taken in by his impersonation of Robert Bond and that he is in Thomas Bond's will. He knows Bond is very wealthy. Jenny will ring this number in London and ask for a message to be passed to "Robert" and say there is a sizeable amount of money in the will for him. We will then time how long it takes him to ring back Jenny. If it is within 24 hours we will know he is keen but if he doesn't ring back then that is that. We will issue a warrant for his arrest and Special Branch will shut down Britain, every seaport and airfield."

"Can I ask how much the lure is?"

"£125,000, stocks and shares, the car and his pick of the champagne and cognac. He knows that there are several bottles of champagne up for auction and in 1958 were valued at £1000 each."

"That is one hell of a lure."

"How bad is Walter's ankle?"

"Not as bad as his temper. It's just his ankle which he wrenched as he skated across the floor out of control."

"I always felt that Walter doesn't really like me."

"Ah well just between us three his father was arrested in Bradford during the 1926 National Strike and badly beaten up by the police so has a bit of a grudge against the boys in blue. Also he sees you as the modern police force. The committee have decided it is time he retired."

"I hope you have enjoyed the tour." Henry then shook hands with Reg and Renton and Frank appeared and showed him back to the Chief's office.

Frank returned and said "How did it go?"

"Prayers were fine and Sykes seems to be a decent sort, let's hope he's the next Chairman of the Joint Committee."

"Did you tell them about the obituary."

"Just outlined the idea, the Chief is keen to get the Redcaps at the house. I shall ring Jenny then let's go and see her and firm up the dates."

35

Obituary

Forty-five minutes later Renton and Frank were in the kitchen at Jenny's house.

Jenny said "I have made some Coronation chicken and sandwiches for lunch so shall we get started on the obituary and all that?"

Renton said "Obituary to come out on 27th November, 9 days time."

Jenny said "In The Times, the Financial Times and in the Daily Express. A small paragraph about the death of Captain Bond."

"Not a local paper like the Yorkshire Post?"

"There is no one here he knows apart from us, Mary and some of the carers."

"I noticed that Arthur White in Knaresborough had the Yorkshire Post in his cafe."

"Well ok, I will include them. What about the funeral?"

"I would include that in the obituary, and donations to the Royal British Legion."

"So when do I ring him about the reading of the will?"

"On the evening of the obituary coming out. The day before you will have two armed police officers living here until he is arrested. They both served in the military police in the war. One is a sergeant and the other a constable in the City of Sheffield Police, Brothers Neil and Alex Walker. They will do the night shift and Ted and Jack the day shift. Are you up to having 4 men here?"

"I have 3 brothers so quite used to men. I am the oldest so had to put up with them for quite a few years."

"I will work out a rota for their food to be brought in."

"Rubbish to that. I will cook and Thomas can pay for the food, what about you? You need to be here to arrest the blighter."

"Well I will see if the Chief will go for that."

The telephone in the hall rang Jenny answered it and said "For you Ralph."

It was Reg. "Can you give DS Jackson a ring, it's not urgent just an update. Here is the number." Renton wrote the number down. He put the receiver down and said to Jenny "Do you mind if I ring Scotland Yard?"

She nodded

He rang the number and identified who he was.

"Hello boss, it's DS Jackson. Just had a call from the sorting office. They have an airmail letter for Miss Ortega. It's from Rio. I told them not to open it and to deliver it which they did. Ten minutes later she comes out and one of my boys followed her and she went to the post office. While she was out we got plod to knock on the door, no answer but he looked through the letter box and could see some boxes stacked up against the kitchen wall. She came back with some shopping. I checked with the post office and it was an airmail letter back to Rio. No sign of Morton. When you nick him give us the all clear to do the address. However if he is on his way to you and we see her leave with luggage we will follow her to the airport and then just as she gets on the plane we'll nick her."

Renton thanked him and put the receiver down and told Frank what was happening. They had lunch and then Renton said "I think we should get back and tell the Chief about the plan to keep the armed units at the house from the 26th November."

Back at the station, Renton rang Margery and asked for an audience, she said 2.30pm would be best.

At 2.30 Renton went into see the Chief to be confronted by Walter Benson sitting there with a pair of crutches.

Margery brought in some tea and biscuits and gave Renton that 'good luck' look.

After a drink and a biscuit and the usual pleasantries the Chief said "I have appraised Walter about the obituary, funeral and the reading of the will. Could you tell us now about the security side at the house prior to the arrival of Morton. He thinks we should involve the Metropolitan Police but I have explained about the Redcaps."

"Yes Inspector" Benson said. "It's important we cover our backs just in case the proverbial should hit the fan. The Mets can carry the can rather than all this flim-flam at Bond's house, it's just poppycock."

Renton was just about to answer when the Chief said "That is enough Walter. We are approaching this in a military fashion, with planning to cover every aspect. Of course you wouldn't appreciate any of this as, if I remember correctly, you were not part of the war due to having flat feet or some other poppycock." The Chief emphasized the word poppycock. "I didn't ask you here for your advice but just to brief you on what will happen."

Benson, looking sheepish, said "Right then. I will go and let you talk tactics."

36

Plan A

The Chief said "I hate it when he calls you Inspector, I have said to call you Ralph, but no matter. So shall we call this Plan A?"

Renton said "The obituary will come out in the newspapers on Wednesday, 27th of this month in the Times, Financial Times, Daily Express and the Yorkshire Post. However, the day before, the Redcaps will move into the house doing the night shift and Ted and Jack the day shift although the day before Morton arrives the Redcaps will be in-situ."

"How is Miss Steel with this?"

"She is up for it, she will do the cooking and has said that it is fitting that the food expenses come out of the victim's wallet, Thomas Bond. Now the funeral will be very low key. Bond's coffin will have the Union Jack on. The obituary will direct any enquiries to the funeral directors. No flowers and any donations should be made to the Royal British Legion through the funeral directors. We are presenting it as a military funeral although there will be no soldiers there. However, David Tinsley is a cornet player with some of Yorkshire's finest brass bands. He will play Last Post at the grave side."

"Police presence at the funeral?"

"Frank and I will be there and of course Jenny, we need you to sanction that Frank and I will be armed from the 27th. We both have permits."

"Of course. Do you think Morton will turn up for the funeral?"

"No I don't think so, there is nothing to be gained. All he will think about will be his inheritance. If he does we will arrest him and if he produces a gun he will have the chance to put it down or be shot. Strategy at the house will be discussed with the others when they arrive. Jenny will leave a message at the house in London about the obituary on the evening of it coming out in the papers."

"Do you think he will turn up unannounced at the house?"

"He doesn't have any keys because Jenny keeps the house keys in her handbag, which is with her at all times. He cannot get in the house, both the front and back door would do the Tower of London proud."

"Well done Ralph I will leave it in your capable hands."

Renton then went down to the incident room and told Frank and Reg about Benson, and the Chief chewing him out. Then he said "The Chief is all ok with our plans so far". Just then Ted walked in.

Ted said "The main fingerprint chap and I served in the Royal Marines during the war. Nice chap. Peter rang him with the details for Morton first thing this morning so when I got there he told me that there is no Michael Morton with that date of birth in their records. So I told him that Morton had enlisted in the war in the Marines but had been seconded into the SOE or some such organisation. His face lit up and he said "I think I might be able to get clearance to access their files, don't hold your breath but I will try. But it might take a week or so to get through the red tape." I gave him Peter's extension number as well as yours and Reg."

"Excellent Ted, imagine if we get proof that his prints are on that syringe. Fingers crossed your pal comes up trumps."

"He said he would prioritise the prints on the needle."

"Righto, I will sort out my notes and I will be in the Red Lion at 6pm. Usual rule."

37

Redcaps

Renton arrive at his usual time and looked at the calendar, Tuesday 26th November 1963. He checked his tray, amazingly there were no files awaiting his approval. Frank came in and said "I see the big news in all the papers is the assassination of President Kennedy."

Renton said "Someone's head will be on the block for that, I see that I have no files today?"

"Busy day today so I had a word with Johnny yesterday and he is going to sign them up. Do we have an actual time the Redcaps are getting here?" said Frank.

Renton said "I was told 11, they can leave their car in the back yard and we take them to the house. The Chief has approved me staying at the house, but to stay in regular contact with him. Once they get here we can brief them on what is going to happen until we arrest Morton."

Frank said "Coffee in Reg's bar?"

"Yes good idea, let's go."

Arriving downstairs they found Steve and Austin talking to Reg.

Austin said "Any word yet on the fingerprints on that syringe?"

Renton said "No, not yet. Thank God Ted mentioned about Morton having been seconded into the SOE."

30 minutes later the telephone rang. Reg answered it and said to Renton "It's for you."

He took the receiver and Jenny at the other end said "I have 2 police officers here from Sheffield."

He said "Can you put the sergeant on?" After a pause he continued "Hello Sergeant Walker. I think our wires are crossed. You are meant to be here at the station at 11am."

"Very good sir we will be there shortly." Came the reply.

Renton handed the receiver to Reg. Once he had put it down Frank said "Bloody Redcaps."

Renton said "Yes and knowing Jenny they will be having a cuppa and some cake or even a bacon roll, we shall see.

One hour later they arrived and were shown to the incident room.

Renton introduced himself and the others, they all shook hands then the Sergeant said "I am Neil Walker and this is my brother Alex."

Renton said "Would you like a cuppa before we talk tactics?"

"No thank you sir, Miss Steel made us one." Sergeant Walker said.

Renton then briefly went through what had happened from finding Millers body.

"So you can leave your car here, transfer all your gear to our car and Frank here will take us to the house and once we have been settled in, we will talk about what is happening from tomorrow. Miss Steel is providing all the food, paid for by her previous employer Thomas Bond who owned the house."

Just then, in walked Ted and Jack. Renton introduced them to Neil and Alex.

Renton said "Ted and Jack will do the day shift and you and Alex will do the night shift. 10am to 10pm to 10am. So let's get to it."

Just then the telephone rang. Reg answered it, then he went into the corridor and shouted "Boss, got the fingerprint chap on the phone, from the yard."

Renton returned and picked up the receiver and identified himself. The voice on the other end said "Hello sir, I managed to get things going on the prints that Ted brought up on Monday and I can positively say that they match the thumb and index finger of the left hand of Michael Morton, date of birth 14th February 1921. I will send you written confirmation of that from the inspector here."

Renton said "Thank you, that is great news and thank you for pushing it through."

45 minutes later they were at the house. Once they had unloaded their gear Jack put their car in the garage.

Renton said to Jenny "I don't suppose I need to introduce you to Neil and Alex?"

"No, we got on fine. They remind me of Ted and Jack, very straightforward, down to earth. I like that in men, a bit like you."

Jenny then gave everyone a tour of the house. Back downstairs in the kitchen she put the kettle on.

She said "My bedroom is downstairs. It includes my office and is en-suite. When Thomas bought this house, it had originally been built by the owner for his large family, so bedroom number 2 for Jack has a toilet and a shower. Upstairs bedroom number 3 is en-suite for Ralph, bedroom number 4 is also en-suite for Neil. Bedroom number 5 is Ted and bedroom number 6 is for Alex. 5 and 6 share a bathroom and toilet. Now meals, breakfast will be cornflakes or shredded wheat and there will be fruit. Lunch, except for Sunday, will be sandwiches. Evening meals will be whatever I can cook up. It could be French or English, who knows?" she laughed. "Saturday mornings it could be bacon rolls which I am partial to but as I am a traditionalist Sunday will be a roast. Washing the pots and preparing the table is down to you chaps. The lounge has magazines, books and there is a games set of dominoes, draughts and chess, oh and I think some playing cards. Over to you Ralph."

"Right chaps, tomorrow Thomas Bond's obituary will appear in various newspapers, but just to make sure that Morton sees it Jenny will telephone the number in London so that the young woman will tell Morton. Whenever that telephone in the hall rings it will be answered by Jenny. In the obituary will be the date of the funeral and its location at Rosehill cemetery. The funeral cortege will come here, pick up Jenny and go straight to the grave, where one of our detectives will play the Last Post. Hearse will then bring back Jenny. Frank will be at the cemetery covertly armed. Originally, I was going to be at the cemetery but I don't want to be seen leaving and coming back in case Morton is watching us. If he turns up here whilst the funeral is in progress then he is to be arrested. We know he could be armed. If he resists with a firearm then you will take the appropriate action."

Jack said "Saves the expense of a trial."

They all laughed and Renton continued. "The date of the funeral is in a week, on the Wednesday and the reading of the will is set for two weeks later on 18th December. Of course there will be no reading. That is the lure to get him here. So show time starts tomorrow. When you do the night shift one of you will be in the garage and there is a tunnel to the garage from the cellar and that will be used at all times for the between shifts. So who will be in the garage for nights?"

Alex put his hand up. "Excellent" said Renton. "Jenny will now show you four the cellar and lead you to the garage."

Neil, Alex, Ted and Jack followed Jenny down the spiral staircase and into the cellar. She put the light on and they all stood there, stunned by the sight of all those bottles of champagne and claret.

Jack said "My God, it's party time."

She led them through to the door that then went into the tunnel and then through the door into the inspection pit to find the light on and Renton waiting for them.

He said "Jack can you show Alex up to the room and the weapon therein?" Jack and Alex went back in to the house. Upstairs Jack showed Alex the Lee Enfield and said "It's not loaded. I'm sure you have used one of these."

They then went back to the others.

Renton said "So on the changeover, whoever is in the garage will come to the house and then the relief will go to the garage. So if you all want to go back to the house and I will see you there." They then returned to the house.

Renton said "Last thing. You can use the conservatory but the blinds are closed just in case we are being watched from the back which looks on to the race course. As we are at the end of November and the nights are drawing in, if you want a bit of fresh air then that will be after 9pm when it is dark."

He then told them the news about the positive identification on Morton's fingerprints on the syringe.

38

Wednesday 27th November 1963

It was the day of the obituaries coming out in the newspapers. Renton had decided that the best position for the day and night shifts would be one person in the room above the garage and one person in the shower room upstairs in the house. They had also worked out the cross fire when Morton would be challenged by Renton on the front step. Jack in the garage, Alex at the corner of the house nearest to the garage, Ted in bedroom number 5, and Neil at the corner of the house nearest to the shed. The plan was that as soon as Morton arrived Jenny would dash upstairs and wave to him from bedroom number 5 and point that she would come down and let him in. Renton would then open the door gun in hand, identify himself as a police officer and for Morton to put his hands behind his head as he was being arrested for the murder of Leonard Miller and Thomas Bond. If he produced a gun then Renton would talk him into the position of putting the gun down. If he took a shot he would be dead before he hit the drive.

After breakfast Jenny went out and picked up the newspapers that would show the obituary. They all looked through the papers. At 1pm Jenny rang the telephone number in London and spoke to the woman on the other end.

"Hello, yes, this is Jenny Steel in Doncaster. I wonder if I could leave a message for Robert. Could you tell him that the obituary for his Uncle Thomas is in the Times, the Financial Times and the Daily Express. It also gives the details of the funeral. Oh yes I will be in all day today and tomorrow but on Friday I will be away from this number until about 6pm. Yes, thank you."

She put the receiver down and went into the kitchen and said "My God. I'm actually sweating and I nearly called him Morton, I think I need a brandy."

Ted said "Are we taking bets on how long before Jenny gets a call from Morton?"

The day wore on and the telephone was silent. Jenny was preparing dinner when the telephone rang.

Renton looked at the clock in the kitchen. 6.20pm.

Jenny went into the hall and answered the telephone "Hello Robert, how are you? Yes, very sad he had a heart attack and the chap at the mortuary said that because of the strokes he was in a very weak state and his heart eventually gave up. It was very quick. Yes, the funeral is on Wednesday, fourth of December at Rosehill. Yes, it will be very low key, just myself, and the Union Jack will drape the coffin. As you know Thomas was not the least bit religious so there will be no service in the chapel. The coffin will come here and then they will take me straight to the grave and I have hired a chap to play the Last Post. Then one of their cars will bring me straight back here. The reading of the will? Yes of course you are in it, the only surviving member for Thomas. Yes I know what he has left you. One hundred and twenty five thousand pounds, stocks and share to the value of about twelve thousand pounds, a bottle of the 1914 Moet Chandon champagne and the Rover. No, there will be no wake after the funeral. Don't forget you have that van to pick up. No, I haven't been in the garage. No, I cannot access the money from the will. Yes of course, best time to ring is say about 5pm any evening. Yes, bye for now."

She put the receiver down and was greeted by a round of applause.

Suddenly the telephone rang again she answered it and said "Yes, just me. No, Mary is finished although she is coming in so we can do all the laundry for the bedding. Yes, he has left me the house and all that booze in the cellar is to be auctioned and the money donated to the Royal British Legion and the RNLI. An advance? No, I cannot give you any money from the will, that is against the law. Well, I have some petty cash about five hundred pounds. Send me a letter with your bank account details and where the bank is, with a letter from you and then I can go to the bank and pay it into your account. The will reading will be here at 11am on Wednesday 18th December, yes of course it will be lovely to see you."

She put the receiver down.

"I think a brandy is in order." Renton said as he handed her a glass of cognac.

She took a sip and said "Do you think he will really come for his money?"

Renton said "You handled it on the telephone perfectly, the fact he asked for an advance means he needs the cash and the thought of one hundred and twenty five thousand pounds in his account will be the lever that gets him here. He thinks to himself he has conned you into believing he is Robert Bond so the rest is easy. I don't think he will turn up for the funeral especially if he gets five hundred pounds in his account. I will warn DS Jackson about the money transfer and see if he emerges from the lair."

Jenny said "The transfer can go ahead without him going to the bank and then the wife or girlfriend can check it for him."

Having finished their evening meal Renton had washed up the pots and dried them, Jenny said "Let me teach you to play backgammon." She made a flask of coffee they were in the conservatory when the telephone rang. Renton looked at his watch. 8.55pm. Jenny went into the hall and said "Hello Robert, 3 telephone calls in one day. Yes I can do that, yes of course. I will just get a pad." She went into her study and came out with a pad. "Hello Robert. Yes, I am ready, fire way." She scribbled on the pad and then said "Yes I have got that. I will go into the bank first thing and do that for you, yes, bye."

She put the receiver down and went into the conservatory. She showed Renton the pad.

She said "It is the main Lloyds bank in the city, just his name and the account number and sort code, all the usual. Not a lot I can do about that.

He could probably telephone them and they would say it had been accepted."

"Tomorrow I will ring DS Jackson before you have the money transferred."

"Because I don't trust him I will transfer it from my secondary account. There is just over five hundred pounds in that account."

Again the telephone rang and Jenny went to it, answered it and said "Ralph, it is for you. It's Frank."

Renton took the receiver and said "Bit late? You still at work?"

"Yes, I decided to do a late shift and have been going through the file with Steve sorting it into some sort of order. Anyway, I got a telephone call from the Chief about an hour ago. He wants you to come in tomorrow at 11am. Apparently some bod from Whitehall wants to see you and the Chief about Morton. It's a Sir Mortimer Farquaharson, my God what a name. He is the liaison officer between the Home Secretary and the Prime Minister, and Special Branch and the M services. Apparently he said to the Chief "It's about this delicate situation you have.""

"Christ Frank. It's beginning to sound very political."

"Yes, what time do you want me to pick you up?"

"It will have to be 9am so you can take me home so I can get my suit and shoes. I'm very casual here."

They both laughed. Then Frank said "9 it is."

Renton put the receiver down and went into the kitchen. Then told Jenny and Ted what was happening.

"Early night for me." said Renton.

39

A Delicate Situation

9am. Frank arrived in his own car and picked up Renton who said "Definitely not a police car." It was a standing joke that Frank drove a car that looked like a rust bucket on wheels.

By 10am they were back at the police station and Renton was suited and booted and ready for the meeting with this Knight of the Realm.

Renton told Reg about the meeting and he said "Yes, I have heard of him. He was the youngest man to become a barrister. Ambassador to some South American country, maybe Argentina or Bolivia, something like that."

Frank said "How do you know all this stuff?"

"My neighbour Geoff Barber, he reads the Times and then passes them onto me, amazing what you can find in there. Inside there is the Royal and what is called the Court news. You cannot forget a name like Farquaharson."

Right on 11am Renton was given the all clear by Margery to enter the Chief's office.

"A ha, Ralph please let me introduce you to my good friend Mortimer". They shook hands and The Chief said "Mortimer this is Ralph Renton, our Detective Chief Inspector. One of the younger up and coming officers we have here in Doncaster."

They all sat down and Renton said "That's very kind sir."

Sir Mortimer said "You know George, I knew Ralph's father, he was a very successful detective himself in London. He had a great reputation for solving murders, some during the war. We crossed swords a few times including the Old Bailey. Shall we get down to business?"

Renton said "I am told that we have a delicate situation."

"Before I tell you about that can you tell me that you have rock solid proof that Michael Morton is your killer for the murders in Yorkshire?"

"We have his fingerprints on a syringe and a small vial both containing aconite in liquid form which was in the bloodstream of the latest victim Thomas Bond. We have no forensic evidence for the other two but with identification parades and evidence from witnesses he can be the only person responsible for their deaths."

"Just the murder of Bond is enough to arrest and charge him then. What about these other two in York and Liverpool?

"They have all the hallmarks of him in the way the victims were killed. All the victims knew each other and he was exacting revenge for his father."

"Michael Morton was trained by the SOE and picked because he was intelligent and spoke several languages. He proved to them he could think on his feet in desperate situations and was a ruthless killer. He excelled in training. Originally SOE agents worked alone from other agents and only knew each other through code names. I'm sure you are aware of this from your work in the war. But he did work with the French Resistance. Another member of the team he trained with and would eventually work with was a Robert Bond. Morton came from a loving family, whereas Bond didn't have that family love. Two very different upbringings but they could have been brothers and both ruthless in what they did for the SOE."

Just then Margery brought in tea and biscuits. After a biscuit and a drink he continued.

"Morton was taken by the Gestapo and the rumour was that he had been sold out by a French agent. He was kept in a police station and tortured for 3 days. But a team led by Bond got him out killing quite a high-ranking SS Major. They tortured him and he told them who had sold Morton out. Bond and Morton then tracked down the agent and his accomplices and killed them all. They were flown back to London, debriefed and then sent back. They did various things but were dropped in Normandy ahead of the D-day landings. After the war SOE was disbanded and various agents were offered positions in certain M services. Bond and Morton declined and went to work with an agency looking for runaway Nazis and then bringing them back to justice. Some of their work was with Israeli teams, principally the Mossad. Morton is still doing that on and off. He and Robert Bond built up a network of agents worldwide to track these people down and it is still going on. They were able to do this thanks to Robert Bond's father who had business connections mainly in South America before the war."

Renton said "Is Robert Bond letting Morton use his name to get close to Thomas Bond so he can kill him? The 5 murders have all happened since Morton came to live with Thomas Bond."

"Brothers in arms I would say." said Sir Mortimer. "It's more than likely that they swapped identities during their work for the Mossad. You must realise that they were working in a country such as Argentina or Bolivia or maybe Chile that is hostile to the English or America. Both those countries have exploited the peoples of South America. They must have had other identities, both fluent in Spanish the main language of that continent. But in 1960 in Chelsea, London, a man was knocked down and killed in a hit and run in the Kings Road. He had a passport and papers for the SOE relating to a Robert Bond and to all intents and purposes he was Robert Bond. However, the post mortem revealed that this man had been a drinker all his life whereas the real Robert Bond may have had the odd drink, but not every day of his life."

Renton said "The victim in York, George MacCrae, was knocked down in a hit and run and died within ten minutes. So who was the man in Kings Road?"

"Fingerprints showed that it was a Ronald Wells. A former soldier fallen on hard times, alcoholic and a few petty crimes under his belt but enough to get him a mug shot and his fingerprints recorded by the police. He had a large roast dinner in his stomach and some whisky. Give him some fresh clothes with a passport and documents sown into the lining of a coat, fill him with food and alcohol and then set him up to die as Robert Bond, giving the real Bond a chance to slip out of the country."

"A coincidence?" said the Chief.

"A coincidence maybe, I think not. A man using the passport of Michael Morton flew to Rio three days after the accident and as far as we know has not returned."

"So that is why you asked me if we have rock solid proof?" said Renton

"Yes, of course. Well I must be going. I am going to York and then Liverpool to see their respective senior officers. It was good to see you George, not long to retirement for both of us."

He shook hands with the Chief and Renton saying "Will you show me the way Ralph, my driver is at the front somewhere."

As they walked down the corridor he said to Renton "Have you thought of transferring to the Mets? With your abilities you could be commissioner material within ten to fifteen years."

"That's very kind of you but my roots are here in Yorkshire and it's nice to see dad's grave so close."

"There is one thing. I am not teaching you to suck eggs Ralph but I would suggest that you hold an identification parade for any witnesses you have. It is the Attorney Generals thing at the moment, he is of the opinion that juries like that sort of thing when they consider their verdict. No smoke without fire shall we say."

Renton showed Sir Mortimer to his car and waved him off in his black Jaguar.

Renton returned to the Chief, who said to him "I bet he said you should transfer to the Mets Ralph."

Renton said "He did actually."

"He tried that one on me 20 years ago when I was a DI. We need you here."

"So how did he know that we are after Morton?"

"I rang Mortimer and asked him to tell us about Morton and Bond. You know what it is like trying to get through the red tape if something has the word secret written on it. We have known each other for years. After the war when I joined the police I thought about Special Branch, thank God I didn't, I much preferred the uniform life. Anyway Ralph, you had better get back to your men."

Renton then told him what he had said about identification parades, no smoke without a fire.

"Yes. I think you should, and if they pick out the right man then all to the better. Of course, if they don't pick him out then the defending barrister will bring that out in court."

Renton went to the collators and said to Frank "Time to take me back. I will explain but first I am famished. Let's go to the diner, lunch on me."

In the Diner Frank said "So apart from telling you all about Bond and Morton's life history, what was it really about?"

"I think he came to us to tell us how dangerous he is and to make sure we had the right chap. Also he wanted to tell us in person rather than on the telephone. Perhaps the brass are of the opinion Morton is too important to go to prison and should carry on catching Nazi's.

"But we are still going to interview him, aren't we?"

Renton said "You bet your sweet backside we are, after all the time we have put in. Interview and charged and then if the brass decide to release him or whatever, that is nothing to do with us."

"Orders is orders, bit like the army "When I shout shit, you jump on the shovel.""

40

Poker

Renton was back in the house and was let in by Ted who said "Jenny has just popped out to get some shopping and that bloody telephone rang. I ignored it of course. That was at 2.25pm and then it rang again at 3pm." They heard a key in the door and in walked Jenny with several bags of shopping. She put them down and then she went out and got a couple more. Ted picked them up and put them on the kitchen table. They heard Jenny pay the taxi driver. She came in, closed the door and took off her coat. Renton had put the kettle on and made them all a drink. Ted then told her about telephone ringing. She said "It could be anyone, let's wait and see. Who fancies a game of poker?"

Ted said "I am up for that, we played the Yanks in the war."

Jenny said "I have some chips somewhere. We can play with them, they are marked in dollars."

She went in the lounge and then returned with a box of chips and a pack of cards.

Renton said "I have played before but I think I am out of my depth with you two."

The telephone rang in the hall. Jenny went and answered it, she turned to the kitchen "It's for you Ralph, its Reg."

Renton took the telephone.

Reg said "DS Jackson has been on the telephone. He said to tell you that Mrs Morton or whatever she is called went to Heathrow yesterday. No luggage, just a handbag. They tailed her and she purchased two singles to Rio. Paid with a huge wad of cash then returned to the flat."

"Did he find out what day they were for and the names on the tickets?

"One ticket for her on the 18th, Susanna Morton, and one ticket for him on the 19th, Michael Morton.

Renton put the phone down and then told the others.

He said to Jenny "What do you think about ringing him up and asking if he is coming to the funeral and will he be staying here the night before?"

She said "Yes why not, but have a large brandy for me afterwards."

They all had a cuppa and a slice of fruit cake and Renton introduced a slice of cheese each.

Jenny said "I haven't seen that for a while, my grandfather always had a piece of cheese with his fruit cake, which was usually left over from Christmas."

When they had finished Jenny went to the telephone and rang the number "Hello yes its Jenny Steel here in Doncaster. Yes, it's about the funeral which is next Wednesday, yes, that is the 4th December. Can you ask Robert if he is coming and also will he be staying the night before, or the night after, or indeed both?"

There was a pause and then she said "I will be here from now on, but tomorrow out after 11am. Yes thank you."

She put the telephone down and went into the kitchen where Renton gave her the brandy.

She said "Right I think we can knock the poker on the head and I will get some dinner ready. I am going to cook beef stew with dumplings and boiled potatoes and cabbage. "

3 hours later and full of food, Renton was washing up when the telephone rang. Jenny went and answered it "Yes, hello Robert. How are you? I was just wondering if you would be staying for the funeral so I could make up your bed ready." There was a pause and she said "Oh no, don't worry. It's all in hand, the funeral directors will pick me up and bring me back. No, if

you are busy then that is fine. Thomas never let anything get in the way of business. Yes, it will be lovely to see you. Yes, the reading will be here in the conservatory starting at 11am. He will probably do all the money that is going to the various charities that Thomas supported. Yes, it's the 18th. Bye for now."

She put the telephone down and said "He said he was in Berlin and won't be able to get back for the funeral, which is very strange because the wireless in the background was giving the 8 o'clock news in English."

"Could be the world service." said Ted.

She said "He didn't ask what time the funeral will be."

Ted said "Because he isn't coming."

41

Funeral

So at last it was the day of the funeral. The night before, Renton had run through what was going to happen. Frank would be a spectator covertly armed putting some flowers on his grandad's grave. David Tinsley would be there, cornet at the ready for the Last Post. It had been an early morning start. Neil and Alex had risen and would be staying up until Jenny was back at the house. Everyone had had breakfast by 8.30am. Ted was at his usual place in the toilet watching the front. The grandfather clock had just struck 10 when Ted said "There is a black Jag coming in the drive and it's being driven by Dennis Parkin in a suit and............." There was a pause and then he said "Bloody hell, it's the Chief and he is in civvies".

It was a standing joke at the police station that the Chief must sleep in his uniform because no one had ever seen him in civilian clothes. The photograph on his desk with his wife was him in uniform.

There was a knock on the door. Jenny opened the door.

"Hello Jenny. The last time I saw you must have been when you were a schoolgirl."

She said "Please come in what a nice surprise but why are you here?"

He said "I thought I could escort you to the cemetery, I know that Ralph and his chaps are tied up and must not be seen at the cemetery and if this bounder Morton is around he will probably think I am your father."

"Well, that is very kind of you." she said

Renton then introduced Neil and Alex to the Chief.

"I would just like to thank you chaps for coming over to help us at this time, much better than having the Mets interfering in our business. I am sure you are being well looked after by Miss Steel." He turned to Jenny and said "I knew your father you know Jenny?"

She said "Yes I believe you were in the same Lodge."

"Yes, yes, well, shall we go. I have telephoned the funeral chaps to say I would pick you up and return you safely home. The coffin will be at the grave at 10.45, so we had better get a move on."

They went to the cemetery and about 90 minutes later Jenny was dropped off back at the house.

Renton said "You were quite a while. Was everything ok.?"

"We were at the cemetery for the time it took to play the Last Post and then he took me to the Danum for a sherry, which is not my favourite drink I have to say. I did see Frank putting some flowers on a grave looking inconspicuous. So I think it's time for a large Scotch."

Renton said "His face when you said that he and your dad were in the Lodge together."

Jenny produced a bottle of whisky and several small glasses and then said "A toast to Thomas Bond, his funeral out of the way and onto the next episode."

They all clinked glasses and knocked back the dram.

The telephone rang. Jenny answered it "Frank for you Ralph."

Renton took the phone and said "Any suspicious people lurking around?"

"No," Frank said, "but when the Chief turned up with Jenny I couldn't believe it. Him in civvies and Dennis looking like a chauffeur, they turned the wrong way for the house."

"Yes he took her to the Danum for a sherry and some polite chit chat. Which grave did you put the flowers on?"

"My grandfather Cyril Franklin Dipper and grandma Abigail Regina Dipper. At the top of the gravestone is the badge of the Coldstream Guards. He was a sergeant major."

"Yes you have mentioned that a few times in the past."

"Really? Oh and the other thing, the Chief wants to see you tomorrow after prayers, he said 11am, he wants to talk about Morton, interviewing him and all that. I shall pick you up 10am in the street just past the house. I will be driving the Ford rust bucket."

"I can't wait."

42

The Fox

The evening meal was finished Renton had washed up and Ted had dried the dishes Jack had gone back to the garage via the tunnel. Jenny said "Anyone for a Scotch."

She poured 3 stiff drinks and then said "I have some paperwork to sort out I will leave you to chat and be back in about 30 minutes."

When she had gone to the study Renton said to Ted "What is all this whispering when Chief Inspector Fox leaves his office?"

Ted laughed and said "Have you noticed he has those metal things on his heels and you can hear them click when he walks."

Renton nodded.

"He has had them for as long as I can remember, right from the beginning that is so the burglars could hear him coming and then they could scarper before he got to them. But he was a DS here and a vacancy came up in the Mets for this anti-corruption unit that was being formed, they were known as the Rubber Heel Squad because you couldn't hear them coming. This was in the fifties and he applied and the Chief couldn't wait to get rid of him. So off he goes. Now the unit was a Detective Chief Inspector, a Detective Inspector and he was one of six detective sergeants. In those days in the Met and I am sure elsewhere certain officers thought that interviewing an offender meant taking your jacket off rolling up your sleeves and then punching the offender in places where the bruises were not obvious. Now they were quite successful tracking down coppers on the take and passing information to the villains. But there were two DC's who had a phenomenal arrest record and the Rubber Heel boys led by Foxy decided to investigate them. He found out their nicknames amongst the criminal fraternity was In and Out. One brought you in and the other knocked you out."

Renton started laughing.

Ted said "No I am serious. Apparently a lot of the villains had been subjected to this technique and sort of expected it. Anyway Foxy found someone who squealed and In and Out went to prison eventually."

"So how long did he last?"

"Two years. He got to DI but started getting death threats, someone kept putting a dead rat in his tray and eventually the bosses thought he should come back. He was eventually offered uniform Chief Inspector which he took. Rumour is he has been used as a rubber heel in the other two Ridings. He always has his office locked, that's why you get his files before he goes on his hols so no one can go prying in his secret files when he's off."

Jenny came out of the study and poured them another whisky.

Renton said "So tell us about your brothers?"

"I am the youngest, eldest brother is Ronnie he was in the Royal navy a commander of a submarine. After the war he married Elspeth an Australian nurse. He vowed he would never want to be near the ocean again and now with Elspeth's brother they own and run a sheep ranch in the middle of Australia well away from the high seas. Reggie trained as an accountant, he was in the Royal Engineers during the war. Now has a small farm in Scotland but is on the verge of selling it and moving to York and will be running Steel Associates from there and bringing in new business. Last of all Robin, he was a pilot with the RAF. He now owns a small air company flying trappers and tourists into deepest Alaska. So what about you two?"

Renton said "I was born in 1919 in Harrogate. My mother was French so after the war in 1920 they went on a late honeymoon in France but both were killed in a car crash. Dad's cousin William and his wife adopted me. So they are the only parents I knew. Dad was a Detective Chief Inspector in the Mets. William Hardcastle eventually became a Detective

Superintendent and very successful at solving murders with his Sergeant Joe Hayhurst. Mum died in 1940. I was intending to go to university in 1937 but instead signed up for the MI6 service, errand boy really. During the war I enlisted in the Intelligence Corps. I ended up in Egypt and being fluent in French helped gathering intelligence initially so we could kick Rommel out. Later I gathered intelligence for the fledgling SAS and LRDG (Long Range Desert Group). Was demobbed in 1945 and joined Doncaster Constabulary and the rest is history."

Jenny said "Very modest what about you Ted?"

"God nothing like that I was born in 1918 my mum and Jack's mum are sisters. I have 3 sisters Jack is an only child. My dad is a collier and I became a collier in 1933 but thanks to the war I escaped the black hole and enlisted in the Royal marines. Jack has more brains than me, don't tell him I said that, and was training to be a surveyor in the pit. He joined up with me and we spent the rest of the war together in the same unit. After being demobbed in 1945 we both joined the police here in Doncaster."

Jenny said "What about Frank, I have heard him mention the Coldstream Guards. He seems very proud of that."

Ted said "His grandfather was a sergeant major in the Coldstreamers, served in Egypt. His dad was also in them in the war in Flanders, the complete regiment was almost wiped out in one battle. So Frank enlisted in them in 1939. He was motorcycle mad and ended up in the Armoured Division. He was wounded but soon recovered and became a despatch rider. He was in his element. Whatever you do don't ask him about bikes. Anyway he learnt very early why they were always asking for volunteers because the Germans used despatch riders as moving target practice. Demobbed in 1945 and joined Doncaster Constabulary."

Jenny said "Bed for me and I will see you in the morning."

Once she had gone to bed Ted said "Grand lass isn't she? I hope you don't mind me saying this Ralph but I think you are in there."

Renton just laughed swigged back his whisky and went to bed.

43

Tactics

The next morning Jenny was up early along with Renton. Ted had made some toast and after everyone had finished Jenny said "I have a taxi coming at 9.30 and hope to get the train to York where I have some paperwork to sign up for one of our biggest investors. I hope to be back by 6pm at the latest."

Ted said "As I am on duty in the house I will make a curry for us all."

The telephone rang. Jenny answered it and said "Ralph, it's for you. Frank."

Renton took the telephone. Frank said "Just to warn you Margery said that the Chief wants to talk tactics."

"I thought we had done all that before, anyway see you at 10. Ted is making a curry tonight is there anything I should know?"

Frank said "Spicy, very spicy."

Jenny left and 30 minutes later Renton was in the street outside the police station when Frank turned up in the rust bucket.

Right on time Renton entered the Chief's office and sitting there was Henry Sykes. They shook hands and Renton said "No Walter today then?"

Henry said "No, it's customary for Walter to spend the Christmas period with his son in Germany and because this weather has been so awful he is going early. A blessing for you and the Joint Committee, he might even get stranded out there."

The Chief turned to Ralph and said, "Could you just run through the deployment of your chaps at the house when Morton turns up on the 18th?"

Renton then ran through what would happen. He omitted to mention that Jack would be acting as sniper from the garage, but just said that he would be one of five people pointing a weapon at Morton. He did say that on the morning in question Frank would be in an unmarked car at the racecourse and Jenny would signal to him when Morton had arrived and then he would drive round to the house and block the driveway in case Morton tried to drive away.

The Chief said "I know that you have proof of his fingerprints on the syringe and vial and proof they are his from Scotland Yard but when he has been arrested what if he refuses to give them voluntarily in the cellblock."

Renton said "We won't press that and he will then think that he has one up on us. Frank and I have talked it over and when we interview him we won't start with Bond we will start with Miller then Wilson. Take a statement with him denying killing them and then approach him about Bond. If he says he had nothing to do with it we will take a statement and hope he signs it and then we will give him the facts of the fingerprints and ask him if he is prepared to commit perjury or admit his guilt. If he does admit his guilt then we will take another statement negating the first one."

"What about the Liverpool and York murders?" said Henry.

"We cannot really interview him about them but we can state that we know about them and the fact that all the victims knew each other from 1914 and worked with each other and about the letters he sent crossing out certain names."

"Very good Ralph. I will let you get back to your chaps. Everything all ok at the house?"

"Yes sir apparently Ted Maynard is cooking a curry tonight."

"Good luck with that."

Renton then went down to the collators and found Frank and Steve with Reg.

He said to Steve "When we interview Morton we will need the exhibits to hand to show him what we have, including the letters where he crosses out the names."

Frank said "So what did he want to talk about if you have already told him?"

"Henry Sykes was there apparently Benson goes to Germany to spend Christmas with his son."

Frank said "His son is a captain in the army guarding the Berlin Wall, hopefully he has more common sense than his father. You never know he might get stranded out there. It's bad enough here this year but out there it will be much worse."

Renton said "That's what Henry Sykes said. Righto you had better take me back chauffeur. But let's go via Dick's Diner. Oh one other thing Frank I need you to make a list of say the best 10 hotels in and around Doncaster to see if Morton books on the day before the reading of the will. In the various names he uses."

Two hours later he was back in the house. Ted said "I swapped with Jack about 1pm and he said at 1.30 and 2.30 the telephone rang, might be Morton."

Renton said "How long did it ring for?"

"Not long, say a minute."

Jenny arrived back at 6.30pm to find that the curry was in the oven, the table was laid and Ted and Renton were enjoying a glass of rosé.

"How very posh." she said as Renton poured her a glass.

"There is another bottle chilling in the fridge for when Neil and Alex come down."

Jenny said "How did you get on with your tactics chat?"

"Henry Sykes was there, it was for his benefit."

Jenny said "My spy in the council offices tells me that Benson will be retiring early next year and that Sykes is a breath of fresh air. Retired Navy bod you know. My brother Ronnie rates him very highly. "Apparently he turned down some sort of diplomatic job to come back here and get into government"

Renton told her about the telephone ringing twice while she was out.

Neil and Alex appeared and Ted said "Right, if everyone is seated I shall bring out the curry, this is the Maynard Madras."

He produced a huge bowl of steaming rice and then 2 large bowls of a very sinister looking curry.

Jenny put out a large jug of iced water and the other bottle of rosé.

"Please tuck in, ladies first of course." Ted said.

Jenny put some rice on her plate and then some of the curry. Everyone was watching her.

She had a taste of the chicken and said, "You know what Ted, that is very nice."

Immediately the men started dishing it out.

Ted said "I do not have any Indian bread but try these buttered rolls with it, they are quite nice.

Everyone agreed and one hour later it was all gone.

Jenny said "You can make that anytime, it was lovely."

As they cleared the pots away the telephone rang. Jenny answered it. She turned to Renton and said "It's the DS in the Mets."

Renton took the phone. "Hello sir. A red Rover was stopped in Sydenham today about 1pm. 2 people in it the driver gave his name as Manuel Garcia from Spain. He had a passport in that name and the necessary documents. The traffic officer only stopped him because he went through an amber light a bit late. He asked him why he was driving an English car and he said it belonged to his good friend Tommy Bond. The officer got back to South Norwood nick and mentioned it to the collator who rang me up. We drenched the area in cars but bloody nothing."

Renton thanked him then told the others. "Frank is going to check out the hotels on the 17th to see if the red Rover is parked nearby. I will ring him tomorrow and give him this name."

44

Quite Unethical

It was Friday morning and there had been another flurry of snow.

Jenny said "I hope we are not getting much more of this or he won't be able to get here on the 18th."

Jack said "He will get here for that amount of money, why don't you wind him up a bit with a reminder of the date?"

"Refresh his memory?" said Ted.

Renton said "Tomorrow is the 7th December and four and a half months ago to the day Miller was killed and here we are waiting to arrest the killer of five men. Perhaps we should have brought the will reading forward?"

Jenny said "No it has to be like this. At 11 o clock I will ring the number and let's see if that gets a response."

At 11 Jenny rang the number, no answer. She put the receiver down. "I will wait 30 minutes, have the Scotch ready."

30 minutes later she tried again "Hello yes could you pass on a message to Robert, this is Jenny Steel. Oh hello Robert how was your latest trip. Oh that is good just a reminder that the reading is on the 18th but we are getting a lot of snow here. Yes, they say it is the worst winter in 50 years it certainly feels like it. Well you have to be present and bring your passport for identification otherwise the solicitor cannot hand you the check and the documents relating to the stocks and shares. No, I cannot advance you anymore money that would be quite unethical and you know I like to do things by the book. Oh, coming here earlier than the 18th."

At this point Renton crept very close to the front door gun in hand. Jenny turned round and Ted also had his gun at the ready and looking through the net curtain on the back door.

She said "Robert you are always welcome to stay, ha ha, and win some money back at backgammon, well unless your game has improved, I think not. If you are coming then give me some notice and I will get some food in and make up your bed. I have washed your shirts and had your jacket and trousers dry cleaned. The house? Yes, Thomas has left that to me in lieu of wages. The van in the garage, I am sure Sam at the garage would buy it off me. No, the Rover is yours, bit bright for me and anyway I always use a taxi and the trains. Yes, well, if you do decide to come early let me know. Yes, bye for now."

She put the receiver down and leant on Renton "God I need that whisky. I nearly called him Michael when he took over the telephone from the woman."

"Same woman? Spanish accent?" Renton said.

"Yes. She sounds more like a Maria than a Deborah."

Ted poured her a whisky which she downed in one.

Renton said "If he wants to come down a few days before the reading then that will be Friday 13th onwards or next weekend. Full alert from now on."

Ted said "If it was me I would come up stay somewhere with 20 miles and then arrive here the day before. But then again I don't think he has a clue his arrogance has convinced him like we said before that he has Jenny fooled."

Renton said "I will ring Frank about 3pm after he has been to the Diner and let him know what's going on."

Jenny said "How do you know he will go to the Diner today?"

Ted said "Regular as clockwork. It's his favourite meal on a Friday, large cod and chips with mushy peas, 2 slices of bread and butter and a mug of strong tea."

10pm, the telephone rang. Jenny answered it and said to Renton "DS Jackson."

Renton took the receiver "Hello boss, sorry about the late call but Deborah Morton or Ortega whatever left the house one hour ago with just a small vanity case, got in a taxi. It's being tailed by half our unit but I put my money on her going to Heathrow. So the plan is they stay with her and don't do anything until she actually steps on the plane and they will nick her and bring her back to South Norwood. I just rang SB (Special Branch) at Heathrow. There is a flight at 11am. She is the only Morton on that flight. The next flight to Rio is on Thursday again at 11am. Hopefully you will get him tomorrow. As soon as my team nick her, we will crash the house. Good luck."

45

I Say, Steady on Old Man

It was 8am on Wednesday 18th December 1963, the day of the reading of the will that didn't exist. Everyone had risen at 6am, showered and was now eating breakfast. The 5 days leading up to this day Frank, Steve, David and Tina had been checking the various hotels within a 20 mile radius of Doncaster looking to see if a Bond or Morton or any Spanish surname had booked in.Nothing was the result. Renton had confirmed with Frank that he would be on the racecourse watching for a signal from Jenny. With him would be Peter and Blot ready to go over the Rover.

Renton, Ted, Neil and Alex had checked their weapons the night before. Jack was itching to try out the Lee Enfield which he said was as good as it was when it came out of the factory.

9am. Renton had rung DS Jackson. There had been no movement at the house in London other than the woman coming out to pick up a pint of milk from the front. They had seen movement behind the curtains but it had been the woman.

DS Jackson said "We haven't seen hide nor hair of any man and when you said that Miss Steel had talked to him then it must be on another line. But once we have executed the warrant we shall find out for sure. Good luck later."

10am. Everyone was on standby. Renton could see the plain car parked on the racecourse road. Waiting and waiting, everyone in the house was waiting for the grandfather clock to chime the hour. Would Morton turn up everyone was thinking. The clock struck 11. Renton looked at his watch to confirm the time. Fifteen minutes later Ted in the bedroom said "He's here."

Jenny then went to the window at the back at the top of the stairs, opened the window and furiously waved a tea towel at Frank. He flashed the car lights and drove off. Jenny then went to the front window, she could see Morton had driven up to the garage turned around and was coming back towards the front door. She saw him look up and she waved to him giving the broadest smile she could. She moved back as if to go downstairs.

Renton was behind the front door, gun in hand. Ted said "He is getting out of the car, he is putting on his overcoat why if he is coming indoors. Left car door open and coming to the steps."

Renton opened the door and held his revolver in both hands, he was rock steady as he faced Morton. He pointed the gun at Morton's chest and said "I am a police officer, do not move."

Morton said "I say, steady on old man I have no cash on me." He coughed and then as if by magic he produced the Colt 45 and pointed it at Renton. To Morton's left Neil appeared, pointing his revolver right at Morton. To the right Alex appeared, also revolver in hand. Morton looked up and where Jenny had been the window was open with Ted pointing a revolver at him. He looked around and saw a car pull into the drive. Frank got out and pointed his revolver at Morton.

Morton said in a very polished accent "I say, surrounded at the ok corral by Wyatt and his deputies. I really don't know what this is all about." He was still pointing the Colt at Renton.

Renton said "I am Detective Chief Inspector Renton and Michael Morton I am arresting you for the murder of Leonard Miller, Ernest Wilson and Thomas Bond." He then cautioned him. Morton said "I think you have got it all wrong I am Robert Bond."

Renton said "In that case you can put that gun down on the floor and put your hands behind your head. If you attempt to shoot that gun you will die and the post mortem will show that you will have at least 4 bullets in you including no head left thanks to a bullet from a Lee Enfield."

Morton said "I see such firepower, I am putting this gun down." He put the gun down on the step nearest to Renton and then put his hands behind his head. Alex immediately came up and handcuffed him with his hands behind his back and then pulled the overcoat down further trapping his arms.

Frank then drove up to the garage, turned round and then came back. Peter and Blot then got out of the car with their bags. Ted appeared and Jack came out of the garage. They then sat in the car with Morton in between them. Renton said to Jenny "Did you ring DS Jackson?"

She said "Don't worry he is taking great pleasure in kicking the door down I am sure. Off you go and be a policeman."

Renton then sat in the front with Frank who then drove them to the police station. In the back Morton said "You are making a very grave mistake Inspector. I will take you to the highest court in the land."

Renton said "Save it for the interview room."

Meanwhile Blot and Peter had started on the Rover and it began to reveal its secrets. Neil and Alex then went indoors. Jenny said "Bacon rolls are the order I think chaps."

46

Suicide Watch

Renton and the others arrived at the police station. Frank drove into the backyard and parked next to the door that led into the cellblock. He rang the bell to let the jailer know that there was a prisoner and also so the station sergeant would be aware and come to the cells. Ted and Jack helped Morton out and into the station sergeant's office in the cellblock.

Sergeant Jim Moss said "Take the cuffs off Ted, he looks a bit uncomfortable."

Renton said "Sergeant Moss, I have arrested this man for the murder of Leonard Miller, Ernest Wilson and Thomas Bond. His name is Michael Morton."

"Not true." Morton said.

"For the time being you will be referred to as Michael Morton as given by the arresting officer." Sergeant Moss said. He then said to Renton "Did you search him when you arrested him, sir?"

"No. Jack did."

"No guns or weapons on him sarge."

Ted took off Morton's jacket and searched it he said "What's happened to the Colt?"

Renton said "I gave it to Blot to document it, it will have to be sent off for a ballistics check."

Sergeant Moss said to Morton "If you could empty your pockets and put everything on the counter and we will then place it in this locked cupboard in a bag."

Morton emptied his pockets.

"The wristwatch as well please." Sergeant Moss then said "four hundred and twenty pounds in your wallet sir and seven shillings and sixpence in loose change. The tie as well we don't want you hanging yourself do we sir."

"Is this all really necessary." Morton said.

Renton said "You must have gone through all this with the Gestapo. The time is now 11.43. You will be placed in a cell and at 12.30 or so you will get lunch. At 2pm I, and two other officers, will start the interview process. But first a detective will come down and take your fingerprints. Also, do you want me to inform a solicitor?"

"No, I am not giving my fingerprints and I don't want some money grabbing solicitor" Morton said.

Morton was put in a cell and Renton said "Who is first for the suicide watch?"

Jack said "Me until 6pm, then Ted until midnight, then Dennis to 6am and then me back and then an eight hour rota. I can't see him doing it but you never know."

Renton then met Frank and they went into the collators.

"So you have him at last." Reg said.

"Yes, first interview at 2pm. He doesn't want a solicitor and he has refused to give his fingerprints."

Frank said "We could get a court order."

"We have a positive on his fingerprints from the Yard and when we get to that with the syringe he will change his tune and want some legal advice."

Frank said "I have sorted out the female cells for the interviews. We haven't had a female prisoner for at least 6 months. The matron's officer has been cleared out into cell F5 so I have a table in there, one chair for him and three for us. So, what's the plan?"

Steve arrived just then "Talking tactics?"

Renton said "Yes, we talk about Miller first that should take up to 5pm. Then tomorrow a full day starting at 10am eventually moving on to Wilson and the Webley and the Lee Enfield being stolen. Jack said that there is EW carved into the stock and Tina confirmed through Marilyn that Wilson told her he had done that in 1916 so a bit more proof of Morton stealing it."

The telephone rang in the cell block. Steve answered it and said, "It's Reg. He's just patching DS Jackson through for you sir." Steve then passed the telephone to Renton.

"Hello," DS Jackson said, "we crashed the house and Ortega is now in custody at South Norwood. In her vanity case there was a diary running from 1914 up to present day. It belonged to William Morton so one of our chaps on Traffic is bringing it up to you. Should get to you in the next couple of hours. It is very interesting reading and you can use it in the interviews. The house was clean but what is interesting is that you can get into the old shop from the flat a hole big enough for a man to climb through. We had OP's on the front and the back but you cannot see the back of the shop. There is a small rat run that comes out of the back of the shop and runs parallel to the high street behind the shops say for about two hundred yards and comes out in a side street. But in the street the door just looks like a billboard. That's how Morton has been getting to the flat and using that telephone. How is he? Is he talking yet?"

"No. Maintains he is Robert Bond, refused to give his fingerprints and doesn't want a solicitor but once we give him the information about his prints on the syringe I think he might want a solicitor."

"Once you get this diary I think that might change his mind. Anyway, good luck."

47

First Interview

Renton, Frank and Steve went into what was now the interview room. Renton nodded to Jack to bring Morton in.

Once Morton had sat down, Renton introduced Frank and Steve. "I must remind you that you are still under caution and that you are entitled to legal advice. Do you want legal advice?"

"No." Came the reply.

Renton said, "Here is a disclaimer to show that you have refused to give your fingerprints and that you do not want legal advice at this time. Could you write your name on the top and then sign it at the bottom."

Morton did as he was asked and then Renton gave the disclaimer to Steve.

"Leonard Miller was strangled on Saturday 3rd August this year in Doncaster library between the hours of 08.30 and 10am. After you had stunned him with a punch you then tied him to his chair and gagged him. Why did you do that?"

Morton said "This is an absolute charade, my name is Robert Bond and I haven't strangled anyone. I have no knowledge of this and if you keep on with this ridiculous question from now on I will just say no comment."

"Very good. I almost believed you but again why did you do this? Did you want to tell him something about his past?"

"No comment."

"Having spoken to Miller you then strangled him from behind, untied him and carried his lifeless body down to the gents. Then bizarrely took down his trousers and sat him on the toilet in the middle cubicle and then jammed this in his throat."

Steve produced the blade and gave it to Renton who said "This is exhibit SB/1 and it is the blade from an entrenching tool that was issued to all the lower ranks on enlisting in the army is 1914 as your father did. You can see on the back of the blade is scratched the initials WM. Your father's initials standing for William Morton. Would you like to say something?"

"Go to hell."

"So where were you on the third of August?"

"I was away from the house on business in Germany. I think for about two weeks. I have an import export business."

"Really, from Streatham no doubt." said Renton.

There was just a small flash in Morton's eyes as Renton mentioned the word Streatham.

"Did you fly to Germany on the first of August or did you go to the Catholic Church behind the library and see the priest and ask him when the library was open at the weekend?"

"No. I flew out on the first."

"The priest gave us a description and if I imagine you sitting here now in the black overalls that are hanging in the garage at the house and wearing the cap comforter you are an exact match to that man the priest spoke to."

"What a load of rubbish."

"Well, we will see what you say after an identification parade. When you were talking to Miller before you strangled him, were you passing on a message from your dear old dad?"

Frank watched Morton clench his fists

"Are you bonkers why would I do that."

"So you do admit that you did talk to him, Miller I mean."

"No comment."

"Did you tell Miller what you were going to do to him after you killed him, I mean pulling down his trousers was that something that happened to your dad in the war, some sort of sexual thing?"

Morton stood up for a second, then sat down and composed himself and said "In your mind maybe."

"We have a statement from someone who saw Miller force your dad to dig a latrine with this entrenching tool. When the hole was big enough he pushed your dad, a fifteen year old boy into it. Your dad put that in his diary. He maybe didn't actually tell you to kill Miller but this could have been the spark that caused you to kill him. What do you think then Michael?"

"Absolute tosh, and my name is Robert Bond."

"Your fingerprints say you are Michael Morton."

"I have never been in trouble with the police and never had to give my fingerprints."

"Yes, we know that you have never given your fingerprints to the police but think back to 1939 or maybe 1940."

"Could I have a glass of water?"

"Yes of course." said Frank. He went out and several minutes later came back with the glass of water which Morton drained in one go.

"Moving on." said Renton "Why jam the blade in his throat after he was dead. You could have just left it on his lap or beside him?"

Morton just shrugged.

"Also, sending your future victims the poppy, was that to scare them? Part of your plan?"

"Sorry old chap but I haven't the faintest what you are talking about."

"Have you figured it out yet Michael? About your fingerprints? Let me explain, all people who are posted to, or volunteer for SOE, have their fingerprints taken. You see a lot of the people who are inducted have a criminal record or give false details, so the SOE need to know who they really are. Thanks to their efficiency and despite your protestations, we know who you really are. I think we will call it a day and let you think about that. But we shall refer to you as Michael Morton until you are charged with murder of three people here in Yorkshire."

Jack locked Morton away and Frank said "There were one or two flashes there where you rocked his boat."

Renton said "Yes. When he stood up I thought he was going to hit me. He may be the tough secret agent who was tortured by the Gestapo but his dad is his soft spot and we shall use that and the prints on the syringe." He picked up the glass that Morton had drunk from and passed it to Steve. "Give this to Peter and see if he can find a fingerprint that matches the prints on the syringe."

Steve said "Can we use that in court?"

Renton said "No, not really but we can give it to him if he keeps on denying it. I think a coffee in the collator's cafe and then home for me."

Twenty minutes later talking to Reg, in walked PC Rowbotham known to everyone as Randy Robotham due to having 4 daughters and 2 sons. "Just had a Met copper come in and give me this for you sir."

He handed a package to Renton who thanked him, Renton pulled out William Morton's diary.

"I will take this home. A bit of light reading perhaps."

Back at the house Jenny had a bath waiting for him. She said "20 minutes to dinner."

After dinner sitting in the lounge with Jenny, while Neil and Alex did the washing up, Jenny said "I have a proposition for you?"

"Oh dear. Am I in trouble?"

"No. Why don't you move in here permanently? You wouldn't be far from the station and you can park your car in the garage and it would be nice to have a man around who I can talk to and who eventually might beat me at backgammon."

Renton laughed and said "Are you definitely the owner now?"

"Yes. I checked the will this afternoon and Thomas has left me the house and some money. It needs some decoration doing and you can help me with the painting. What do you say?"

"Well after much thought I will have to say yes."

"Fantastic" said Jenny "Shall we seal the deal with a whisky when the boys have washed up. Also I am going into Doncaster tomorrow to see the solicitor for Thomas and he will formally read out the will and that will be that."

Just then there was a knock on the door and Neil and Alex came in.

Jenny produced 4 glasses and poured a generous tot into each and said "A toast to a job well done......almost."

After they had knocked back the whisky Neil said "We have sorted out our gear and will go in with you tomorrow, do our statements and then return to Sheffield if that is okay with you."

"Certainly" said Renton. They then went back into the kitchen and Jenny said "So what is in that package you brought home?"

Renton smiled and said "Home, I like the sound of that. This is the diary of William Edward Morton which he started in 1914 and then passed on to his son Michael, who continued it up to being arrested by me. Shall we have a look."

Jenny moved closer to him on the settee.

30 minutes later she said, "My God he didn't pull his punches about Miller and the others."

Renton said "Look at the writing of a fourteen old boy, it starts as a scrawl but it improves as time passes on. There is an index of addresses at the back. I asked Arthur White if he knew where Morton might be living and he said he had no idea. I am sure he knew."

48

Second Interview

Frank picked up Renton, Neil and Alex and they arrived at the station at ten past nine. They all went into the collators where Reg found Neil and Alex the appropriate paperwork for their statements.

Frank looked at the diary and said "Juicy is it?"

Renton said "He didn't pull any punches, I can tell you. Have a read and then we will have him out at ten."

Right on 10 Morton was brought into the interview room by Jack.

"Good morning Michael did you sleep well?" Frank asked.

"My name is Robert."

"Now, you seem to have someone who can furnish you with passports in any name. For instance, what about the ex-soldier that you set up? You ran him over in Chelsea and then made it look like he was the real Robert Bond. The real Robert Bond then went abroad three days later with a passport in the name of Michael Morton, but with Bond's date of birth."

"Look old chap this is all a bit far-fetched I haven't the foggiest what you are burbling on about."

Renton then said "Look at this photograph, one of the many that Miller took. This is exhibit JB/1 can you see this chap here?" Renton pointed to MacCrae.

"There is your dad to one side, what age would you say? Fourteen, maybe fifteen? He is not looking very happy would you say. In fact in the photos with your dad in he isn't smiling in any of them. Good reason is because at some stage around this time MacCrae tried to rape your dad in the stables with Ernest Wilson close by looking for sloppy seconds."

Renton watched Morton clench his fists and swallow very obviously.

Renton continued, "But the diary your dad kept is here. I produce this as exhibit AJ/1 it says "I was in the stables with Mac clearing up the shit ready for when they stabled the horses. As I turned round Mac grabbed me and turned me round and bent me over the gate. I could feel him trying to pull my trousers down he had one hand on my neck and said "It's time to lose your virginity boy." I cried out and some of the farriers ran in and dragged him off me. I pulled my trousers up and ran out nearly knocking Wilson over. He cuffed me as I went by.""

Morton said nothing.

Renton said "How does that make you feel Michael? I am sure you have read that in the past, but here we are nearly fifty years later reading what this poor child had written on that day."

"What does that have to do with your murder investigation?"

"Revenge Michael. The run up to the murders and what took place when you told Miller who you were and what you were going to do to him reeks of revenge."

"Very dramatic I must say." said Morton.

"Let's talk about Ernest Wilson who was waiting his turn with your dad after MacCrae. We have two witnesses who are prepared to come to an identification parade and I am sure they will pick you out as the man enquiring at the Lucky Horsehoe Riding Stable asking about riding lessons for his niece. They described exactly the clothes you were wearing at the time and are now in the wardrobe at the house. They fancied you those two women so were very particular in describing you."

"Lucky them."

"So you went back very early on Sunday the 8th September this year and murdered Ernest Wilson. Same MO as Miller. Creep in, stun him and then tie and gag him to a chair and tell him what you are going to do to him after death. Did he say something aggressive because you made him eat horse manure which was in his throat and mouth. Just strayed from the MO I thought. You did all this talking to the victim in Liverpool with Edward Webb and you didn't have much time to talk to MacCrae but you said a few well chosen words no doubt.

Morton said "Is that a question or are you just rambling?"

"Then you stole a Webley pistol and a Lee Enfield rifle. Did you also steal the Napoleonic bayonet that you used to kill a defenceless man in a wheelchair? What terrible thing did he do to your father to warrant that? Oh, let's look in the diary. Touched him up and threatened him with a knife and a bayonet, made him cry."

"Enough. When are you going to stop going on about this stuff from that diary."

The three of them watched him wringing his hands together.

Renton said "When you stop this charade and admit that you are Michael Morton the son of the man that wrote this diary. From the fifties it is your writing in here. It looks very much like the writing on the disclaimer that you filled in and signed. Quite elegant compared to a teenager's scrawl."

"I have had enough just. Leave it for God's sake."

"Righto" said Renton "I think we will take a break for lunch and be back for 2.30 when we shall talk some more."

"Can I ask for something?" said Morton.

"Can you get me a Financial Times from my money the sergeant has?"

Renton said "Yes of course."

Once he was locked up Renton said "To Dick's Diner via the shop."

49

Third Interview

Back from lunch, Renton was talking to Frank and Reg. Peter came in and said "The car is completely clean of fingerprints but behind the front passenger seat was this." He handed Renton a satchel type briefcase. Inside was a Webley pistol and a small box of bullets and a couple of clips of ammo for the Colt. "The revolvers and the rifle will be going away for analysis to see if they have been used in any crimes."

Renton pulled out a wallet. Peter said "£2000 in that." Renton then pulled out a familiar large brown envelope with photographs in and paperwork relating to the shop in Streatham and some insurance documents and a small envelope. He opened it and read the letter. It said, "Son, whatever you do to those five bastards I am in total agreement and you have my blessing. Love you. Dad." He passed it to Frank.

Frank read it and said "If that is not an endorsement I don't know what is."

Peter said "There was also this in the glove compartment." He handed Renton a small velvet pouch with a red ribbon round the neck.

Renton opened it and poured out 7 small diamonds, each a bit bigger than a grape. Frank whistled "My God how much are they worth?"

Renton said "I need to make a telephone call." He rang jenny and said "Did Thomas have any diamonds in the house in the wall safe maybe?"

She said "Yes he kept them in a small velvet pouch with a red ribbon round the neck. I will have a look." Several minutes later she came back and said "It's gone from the tray."

"Yes. Peter has found them in the glove compartment of the Rover, see you later."

As he put the receiver down he heard Jenny say "Thieving bastard."

"Righto Frank. I think it's time to give him the good news about having his prints on the syringe and see what he thinks of that."

Fifteen minutes later they were sitting in the interview room with Morton.

Renton said "Here is exhibit RR/1. As you can see it is a cigar box and inside is this." He opened the box to show the syringe and the small vial. "Have a good look Michael." Renton closed the box and gave it to Steve.

"What do you think of that then Michael?"

"You like to get high occasionally inspector?"

"That box was found in a small tunnel running from the inspection pit in the garage towards the house. Also, the vial and the syringe contain a highly poisonous liquid, a derivative of aconite. That same liquid was found in the bloodstream of Thomas Bond and the only person that could have administered it was you Michael, just before you went off on one of your alleged trips."

"This is all a bit James Bond. Have you seen the film? It's very good. Of course I am no relation."

"Let us now talk about your alleged trips away from the house. Here is exhibit FD/1 so DS Dipper here will read out the day you committed a murder and then read out the days you were not at the house. Frank, over to you."

Frank said "Edward Webb, died 5th November 1961. Away in Germany 1st to the 15th. Then we have MacCrae, run down 3rd February 1963, you were in Spain 27 January to 17th February. Then Miller, 3rd August this year but you were in South America 28th July to 22nd August. Lastly Wilson, killed on 8th September but you were away 1st September to 15th September in Germany."

"I was away a lot on business, making money."

"If you were away making money then why ask Miss Steel for an advance from the will?" Renton asked.

"No comment."

"I must tell you that Miss Ortega or Morton whatever she is, is in custody in London having been arrested with 2 single tickets to Rio when you were due to fly out today. She might be released but that all depends on Michael Morton, not Robert Bond. Oh here is your Financial Times. You will be able to look at your stocks and shares when you are in prison. We will finish the interview now. "

As they all got up to leave Renton said to him "The prints on the syringe and the vial have all come proved to be your prints for the Michael Morton who joined the SOE all those years ago. Think about that until tomorrow when we are on the fourth interview. Take him away Jack."

Renton said to Frank "An early finish for me. Can you check the Redcap's statements and then add them to the file. Fourth interview tomorrow at 10am.

Later that day, Renton had just cleared way the pots after dinner in his new home when the telephone rang. Instinctively he looked at his watch. It was 7.45pm. He went and answered it, it was Ted.

"Hello boss. Morton asked me to ring you to say he would like his barrister, not a solicitor, informed he is here and would like him present for all future interviews. Change of heart maybe?"

"Yes our parting shot was that we had his fingerprints on the syringe."

"He said the barrister's name is Giles Wentworth-Sergeant and he can be found at Lincolns Inn Fields and his personal telephone number is in his diary that you have."

"Righto. I will find the number and ring him now and see if we can get him down tomorrow, pass that on to Morton."

"No sweat boss."

Renton looked through the diary and there in the back were two numbers for him. The first one in brackets had Lincolns I F. Renton rang the number and a man answered the call. Renton asked to talk to Giles Wentworth-Sergeant. The voice at the other end said "That is me, and why at this late hour?"

Renton then told him about Morton and that he had been interviewed declining legal advice but had now changed his mind.

The barrister said "I doubt I can get a train to the North now. I shall drive. Is there somewhere secure at your station for my car?"

"Yes of course." Renton said.

"In that case I shall be with you all being well. Eleven o'clock prompt."

Renton put the receiver down and then rang Frank at home.

"Bit posh." Frank said.

50

Fourth Interview

Renton arrived at the police station at 8am. He checked his tray and then went down to the collator's and made himself a mug of coffee. He looked over the Redcap's statements and then rang DS Jackson in London.

"Hello Guvnor, how is it going?"

Renton then told him what had happened so far. He then told him about the barrister.

DS Jackson said "Tricky bastard. Very successful. He is actually part of the law team for the M Services so he probably knows Morton quite well. If you tell him up front what you have on matey boy he might just make him come across."

Renton told him about the two telephone numbers against the barrister's name.

"I reckon the second number is probably the law team in the M building. I will check it out and get back to you."

Renton put the receiver down just as Reg, Frank and Steve walked in.

Renton said "The barrister is called Giles Wentworth-Sergeant and is arriving at 11am and would like to park his car in the rear car park for safety. Steve, if you can meet him and then show him into the car park and then in through the front office to the cells. I am sure he will want a chat with Morton first and then we will have a chat with the barrister and then go into the fourth interview and see what happens."

Frank said "What are you going to tell the barrister exactly?"

"DS Jackson said he is a tricky bastard and is part of the law team for the M Services and probably knows Morton, perhaps from the past. He did say that if we tell him what we have on Morton he might get him to talk. Who knows?"

10.55am. Frank and Renton were in the CID office looking down on the rear car park as Steve guided the barrister in.

Frank said "Jesus! An Armstrong Siddeley, one of the burgundy ones, the Lancaster model too. Very nice and worth a few bob too."

Renton said "Righto Frank. Let's go and meet him in the cellblock."

As Steve brought him through the front office into the corridor that would lead to the stairs down to the cells, Austin was coming the other way. He stopped and said "Wentworth, how are you?" The barrister stopped and thought for a moment and said "Good God. Austin Bradley, how the devil are you?" They shook hands "Still not a copper surely?"

Austin said "No, retired but I pop in occasionally and see if I can help, old habits die hard. My son Jack is the jailer today."

Steve and the barrister carried on to the cell block. Steve introduced him to Renton, Frank and Jack.

Renton said "Would you like some time with your client."

"Well actually I could murder a cup of tea, no sugar and we have a chat first if that is alright with you."

Jack went off and made him a cup of tea. He returned and the barrister said "Jack, I understand your father is Austin Bradley who I have just met upstairs?"

"Yes," said Jack. "How do you know him?"

"I was a very young and foolish officer in the trenches and Sergeant Major Bradley looked after me and taught me how to survive and treat men as equals."

"Sounds like dad." Jack said.

One cup of tea later sitting in the interview room the barrister said "I believe in being fair to all parties and I like the truth from both sides so tell me what Michael has done and we shall sort it all out. But please call me Wentworth, everyone does."

Renton then told him about the three murders in Yorkshire and that Morton was wanted for two more out of the county and would have to be transported there to be interviewed by them as well.

"I see. Bring him in now Jack and I will have a talk to him alone."

Jack brought Morton to the interview room as Renton, Frank and Steve walked out. As he pushed the door almost closed they heard Morton say "Hello Giles, so good to see you."

Forty five minutes later the barrister beckoned Renton and the others to come in they sat down and the barrister said "Michael has something to say".

Morton said "I am Michael Morton, the son of William Edward Morton."

Renton said "I see. Let's talk about Thomas Bond." He motioned to Steve to pass the cigar box which had been in the garage. Renton undid the ribbon opened the box and showed the barrister and Morton the syringe and the small vial.

Renton said "This is exhibit RR/1. On the syringe and the bottle are two fingerprints. The fingerprints were taken to Scotland Yard to their National Fingerprint Bureau where they were positively identified as belonging to you Michael, from when your prints were taken when you were seconded into SOE. Inside that syringe and vial is a liquid which is a derivative of aconite, highly poisonous. Did you inject that into Thomas Bond on the day before you left his house on the 14th of September this year?"

"Yes I did."

"Where did you inject this liquid into his body?"

"Just above his ankle, I cannot remember which ankle."

"Why did you decide to kill Thomas Bond.?"

"He and four other people in the First World War made my father's life hell for four years. They subjected him to bullying and sexual abuse. He kept a diary which you now have and when he died that diary was passed to me. I decided that one day I would find them."

"Just before we continue onto Miller can you explain why you stole these?"

Renton then pulled out the small velvet pouch and took out the seven diamonds. "These are exhibit PJ/3."

"I decided that he would be dead very soon and I had more use for them than him."

"How did you know they were in the wall safe?"

"Thomas told me."

Renton put the diamonds back in the pouch and then into the exhibits file box.

"Now let's move onto Leonard Miller. He died in Doncaster Library on Saturday the third of August this year. You strangled him didn't you?"

The barrister then said "From what you have told me about this murder, you have no real hard evidence to prove that Michael killed Miller."

Renton said "I would still like to question him about it.

The barrister said "Then I suggest from now on that Michael will reply with no comment."

Renton said "Michael on the Thursday before you murdered Leonard Miller you went to the nearby Catholic Church and you asked the priest for the time the library opened on the Saturday didn't you?"

"No comment."

"If necessary I could call for an identification parade and put you in a line up of similar men to you and I am sure that priest would pick you out. He is a very credible witness."

Wentworth said "That is up to you Chief Inspector but at the end of the day a judge and jury will want some tangible proof, now known as forensic evidence such as fingerprints or similar."

Renton said "Very well. I shall continue. What about Ernest Wilson? You strangled him as well on a Sunday but on the eighth of September this year."

"No comment."

"We have two witnesses who have made statements describing you as going to the stables and making a bogus enquiry about riding lessons for your niece. Once again I could call an identification parade and this time the witnesses would pick you out."

Wentworth said "Once again Chief Inspector that is up to you."

Renton said "However the clothes you wore that day were hanging up in the wardrobe in your bedroom at Thomas Bond's house and I have them here as exhibit RR/2". He then showed them to Wentworth and to Morton. "Are these your clothes?"

Morton looked at Wentworth who shook his head.

"No comment."

"In the red Rover you have been using, a Webley pistol was found with ammunition for it. Do you accept that?"

Before the barrister could say anything Morton said "Yes."

Renton said "That pistol and ammunition belonged to Ernest Wilson, I have the paperwork to show that it belonged to him from 1915. Also in the garage at Bond's house we found a Lee Enfield rifle and ammunition. The only person who had keys to the garage was you, isn't that correct?"

"Yes."

"Was the rifle yours?"

Before the barrister could intervene Morton replied

"Yes, I am a collector of pre-war weapons."

Renton said "But that rifle belonged to Ernest Wilson and you stole that from him along with the Webley pistol didn't you?"

"No comment."

"Did you enjoy killing him?"

"No comment."

"Some sort of a perverted wish for revenge I think."

Morton said "Why don't you fuck off. You have no idea what my dad went through with those bastards."

The barrister said "Calm down Michael. They are just trying to goad you. Can you just continue with the questioning please Chief Inspector?"

"Certainly. I am not going to question you on the murders in Liverpool and York but those murders and these murders are all linked. Each victim prior to being murdered received a British Legion poppy. Was that to get them to panic, to perhaps twist the knife?"

"No comment."

Renton said "Now just cast your mind back to Tuesday 6th August. You were in a village called Campsall not far from here and you were changing a tyre on the Rover. Do you remember that?"

Again before the barrister could intervene Morton said "Yes. I remember it was a lovely day."

"You were approached by a chap known locally as the pig man. He collected scraps from various cafes for his pigs. He came and chatted wanted to see if you needed a hand and during your conversation you offered a cigar. This one I produce as exhibit JB/1"

The barrister said "This is totally irrelevant, I think it is time to stop this comic routine."

Renton looked at Morton and said "Well?"

"No comment."

Renton said "You was wearing a set of black overalls, a cap comforter and black boots which I produce here as exhibit RR/3. These were hanging up in the garage of which the only person who had the key was yourself. would you like to comment?"

"No."

The barrister said "I think we can leave it there. Michael has freely admitted to killing Thomas Bond but the other two cannot be proved because as I have said, you have no hard evidence."

"Yes and because of that we will be having an identification parade tomorrow which I think is relevant to the killings of Miller and Wilson. We have three witnesses."

"Yes. If I could have a few words with him now?"

"Of course."

Renton and the others left the interview room. Renton said to Steve "I want you to type out the interviews showing all those present including the ones before the barrister arrived then tomorrow we will ask Morton and the barrister to read through them and they can sign them as a true account."

Frank said "What about getting him in court?"

"We will keep him here if the barrister is okay with that and then into court on Monday and conveyed to prison straight after."

Ten minutes later the barrister came out and Renton explained about keeping Morton in the station after charging and appearing in court on Monday.

Wentworth-Sergeant said "What about him going to court tomorrow and then on remand?"

Frank said "There's no court tomorrow and we will be having the ID parade then anyway."

"But what about prisoners you might arrest tonight? Wouldn't they go to court tomorrow?"

"No they would be kept in until Monday."

The barrister told Morton what was happening. Morton was locked away and the barrister was shown out by Steve.

Ten minutes later the front office constable came in and said to Renton "Excuse me sir but there is a lady in the front office called Mrs Walpole and you need to hear what she has to say about cap comforter man. You need to get a statement."

Renton turned to Steve and said "Let's go and bring some statement forms."

Five minutes later they were sitting in the broom cupboard with Iris Walpole.

Renton introduced himself and Steve and said "Mrs Walpole, what would you like to say to us?"

"I have been away looking after my mother in Preston since the beginning of August."

Renton said "I trust she is well."

"Oh yes. She is a tough old bird. She was 93 three weeks ago, I'm 73 now."

"You look very well if you don't mind me saying so, what do you have to tell us?"

"So I came back 3 days ago, I live in Tickhill. So yesterday I went to see Doris my good friend Doris Jenkins and she told me about poor Leonard and that he had been murdered by some chap in one of those woolly army caps like my Ronnie used to wear in the war, bless his soul, died in 1950. Anyway, Doris is the cleaner at the library and on the Saturday, er, let me think, yes the 3rd August the day poor Leonard died I thought why don't I surprise her and meet her at the library and we could go for dinner. I know she sometimes meets Alice Ramsbottom, we all went to school together. So I got there just after nine, maybe twenty past nine and I looked through the fire door because the library doesn't actually open until ten o clock."

"Did you see anything inside?"

"No. I thought perhaps Leonard was having a wee and I couldn't see Doris so I thought I would wait a bit and then all of a sudden this man in black overalls came out he looked a bit flustered and he was really sweating. Well I mean wearing a woolly hat, and in August. I said "Are you alright dearie, you look in a right mucksweat." He said "Yes thank you. I am fine." Very posh voice I thought. I said "Have you seen Doris the cleaner?" He said "No she left about an hour ago." So I walked off and went towards the town and stopped for a cigarette and then I saw him driving a black van, you know one like Bernie Hopwood has, the pig man, only this one was black."

"Can you describe him, how tall was he?"

"The same as my Ronnie I would say six foot, broad shoulders, good looking and he had some posh aftershave on, nice smell, covered up all that sweating."

"What was he wearing?"

"Black overalls and that green woolly army hat and as I looked back he had those black army boots that soldiers wear. When I looked back he lit up a cigar, very nice I thought not cheap I should say."

"Mrs Walpole. If he was in an identification parade with ten other men would you be able to pick him out?"

"Oh yes. He had that Gregory Peck look and about the same age I would say."

"We might do a parade tomorrow, might be about eleven to twelve midday is that okay?"

"Yes of course dearie."

"Righto. Steve here will take a statement and we will get a police car to pick you up and take you home."

"Oh how nice. No need for a lift home though, I will meet Doris and Alice for lunch."

Renton left Steve and then found Frank and told him about the statement.

Frank said "Bloody marvellous. So we have him at the place of the murder just after he topped Miller."

Renton said "Once Steve has finished see if David Tinsley can find 12 or so lookalikes, for tomorrow at eleven. What's the going rate?"

Frank said "One pound and ten shillings an hour or part thereof. I will go and look for David now."

Renton said "I will have great pleasure in telling Wentworth a bit later on. Let him have lunch first. Can you contact Marilyn Cooper and Freda Williams at the stables and Father Dominic and have them down here tomorrow for say ten thirty."

Peter came up to Renton and said, "Sir, about that glass, a thumb and fingerprint exactly match the prints on the syringe."

Renton said, "This gets better by the minute."

51

Identification

Renton arrived at his usual time of 8.30 am. The calendar was showing Saturday 21st December 1963. He checked his tray and saw that DI Johnny Martin was still sorting out his crime files. He had a quick run through the 3 in his tray and signed them up for court. Because Christmas was so close the courts would only be in operation until the 23rd so these files would now be tried after Christmas. He checked to make sure the offenders bail notice matched their dates for court.

He found Frank in the CID office and said "Any luck with the stooges for the ID parade?"

"Yes we have 12 coming in at 11am. I helped David out and they are a good match. It'll be interesting to see what the barrister makes of them. What did he say when you told him?"

"He wasn't happy because he was having a snooze after lunch. He objected of course, short notice and all that guff, and he is going to complain to the Chief and the Attorney General. We will have all four witnesses in the new witness room. Father Dominic first then Mrs Walpole then Marilyn Cooper and lastly Freda Williams. Once they have done the ID they will then be taken to the canteen by Peter and DS Moran will take a short statement from them about which number they picked. Steve will then bring down the next one, then to the canteen and so on. We don't want them mixing and saying which number he was although I think Wentworth will get him in different positions.

They went down to the cellblock and found the duty inspector Bill Hornby and the station sergeant Matt Smith sorting out where to have the parade. There were no prisoners in at all except for Morton so they decided to have the parade in the sterile area between the cells which was wide enough for 12 men to stand in a line if necessary.

Inspector Hornby said "I will conduct the parade." He looked at Renton and said "You and Frank stay upstairs out of the way. When the barrister has stopped fiddling about we'll start."

Renton explained to Bill about who was doing what.

Everyone agreed. Renton and Frank went to the collator's. Once there and drinks made, Frank said "We couldn't have a better pair with Bill and Matt doing the parade."

Renton said "We just need him picked out."

11am arrived and in the cell block were eleven men who were all of a similar appearance but all dressed differently. Morton had a shower and dressed. Because Morton was wearing a suit when he was arrested he was given a jacket to wear with his suit trousers. Wentworth wanted all of them to have an open necked shirt. In the line up was Blot and Johnny Martin along with 10 other men. Wentworth decided to have a total of 9 men in the line up and number 6 was Morton. When Wentworth was satisfied with the line up he said to Steve to bring the first witness down.

Father Dominic came in and had a good look and said to Bill "Definitely number 6."

Wentworth had Morton hold number 3. Mrs Walpole picked him out "Oh dearie number 3." she said to Bill.

Morton then became no.9. Marilyn Cooper came in and said "The handsome one. Number 9."

Morton then became number 1. Freda Williams came in and said "That creature. Number 1."

When the last witness had gone Renton came down to the cell block. Bill Hornby said "Four positive idents."

Renton, Frank and Steve went into the interview room and waited for Morton. He was brought in by Ted and Wentworth.

Renton said" Michael, as you now know you were picked out by two witnesses related to the death of Leonard Miller who you killed. Would you like to say anything about that?"

"No comment."

You were also picked out by two witnesses from the stables where you killed Ernest Wilson. Do you wish to say something about that?"

"No comment."

Renton then said "You will be charged this afternoon at 4pm and then kept in custody until court on Monday at 11am. You will then be remanded to prison and at some time will be interviewed by officers from York and Liverpool. To save you being transported back and forth those officers will come to the prison on Tuesday the 24th."

Wentworth said "I will just see Michael for a few minutes."

Renton and the others left.

Wentworth came out as Ted took Morton back to his cell "I will be back at 3.30pm. As for the interviews at the prison, we shall see about that."

Steve escorted Wentworth out of the police station.

Renton said to Steve "Do you have the interviews all ready for the barrister to look at?"

"Yes sir."

"Righto. Lunch break now I think. Then back at 2pm here in the murder room. I have a couple of phone calls to make." In his office Renton then rang DI Bob Williams in Liverpool and DI Bill Reynolds in York. He told them about the positive identification and that he got the impression that the barrister wasn't happy about Morton being interviewed in prison.

Bill Reynolds said "To be honest, because it is Christmas Eve I think the prison will refuse and say come after."

At 2pm he was back in the murder room with Frank and Steve.

Renton "So we show Morton and the barrister the statements of interview, by the way Steve did you type them all or get Reg to do them?"

"No sir, I bribed Peter."

"So show them and then see if Morton and Wentworth will endorse them. If he doesn't then I will make a note in my diary. Coffee time now though, and force Reg to get the biscuits out which I know he has."

From the collator's a voice said "Jammy Dodgers."

3.30pm. Renton was in the charge room with the station sergeant. Steve showed in Wentworth who then read through the interview statements. He said "I will endorse them Chief Inspector."

At five minutes to four Ted brought Morton to the charge room. They were both laughing as they came in. Wentworth said "In good spirits Michael?"

Morton said "Yes. Ted and I were just talking about the aftermath of D-Day, we were both in the same village at the same time in 1944."

Just then, in walked the Chief. Renton introduced him to Wentworth and Morton, they didn't shake hands. Renton then charged Morton with the killings of Leonard Miller, Ernest Wilson and Thomas Bond. After each caution Morton made no comment. The Chief left and then the station sergeant explained about Morton staying in police custody until he appeared in court on Monday. Ted took Morton back to his cell.

Wentworth said to Renton "Do you know where I can get a decent roast tomorrow. The food is very nice at the Danum but just a bit too fancy for me?

Renton said "Well, DS Dipper and I got to the Red Lion pub. Very decent roast and a nice pint of bitter but you need to get there at 12 or go in this evening and book a table."

"Very good I might see you in there."

Steve showed Wentworth out of the station and returned to the collator's.

Renton said "Let's call it a day for now and tomorrow we need to have a working file ready for court on Monday along with the exhibits because DS Jackson said Wentworth is a tricky bastard and you never know what he might try on in court."

Frank said "Can you believe that it is exactly 5 months since Miller was murdered?"

Renton said "I think we did rather well to get it sorted in 5 months, a couple of murders I have worked on in the past have taken a lot longer and we found Liverpool and York's murderer for them."

52

Court

It was 11am on 23rd December 1963. Renton, Frank and Steve were in court no.1. The jailor brought Morton into the dock. The clerk of the court said "Are you Michael Morton of no fixed address at this time?"

Morton said "That is correct."

The clerk then read out the charges and said "How do you plead to unlawfully killing Leonard Miller on 3rd August 1963?"

Morton answered "Guilty."

The clerk read out the other charges and Morton pleaded guilty to those as well.

Wentworth made no reasons for bail and Morton was remanded to prison. He was then taken to the court cells and taken to prison by 3 very large warders.

Renton said "I wonder why he pleaded guilty to all three?"

Frank said "Get it over with I reckon, and then plead not guilty to Miller and Wilson when it gets to the Old Bailey next year.

Renton said "Might as well be done for a sheep instead of a lamb, or something like that."

Back at the police station they went into the murder room to find everybody there, even Austin.

Reg said "The Chief asked me to get all the team together."

Everyone had made themselves a drink followed by Renton, Frank and Steve. Reg made a short telephone call and several minutes later the Chief walked in with another senior officer. Everyone stood up.

The Chief said "Please sit down you chaps and you of course madam." He looked at Tina, she blushed.

He continued "First of all I would like to thank you all for the sterling work that you have put in since the 3rd of August, five months since we found Miller's body in the library. So give yourself a clap."

When they had finished he said "I would like to introduce Chief Superintendent Archibald Duckworth who will be taking over from me in March when I retire. He has an incredible track record and I am sure you will make him feel at home. Also, in the New Year Detective Chief Inspector Renton will become Detective Superintendent Renton." There was a round of applause. "Also, there will be Detective Inspector Frank Dipper." Another round of applause "and Detective Sergeant Stephen Bowers." A third round of applause. "I don't know if you know but Ted Maynard was promoted to sergeant several weeks ago and he has been keeping very quiet. I understand there is a tradition of an open wallet to celebrate in the Red Lion. To that end I have put twenty five pounds behind the bar for 6pm. First come, first served. Thank you. To another final round of applause, the two Chief's left the room.

Renton then said "I have moved into the house with Jenny Steel." There was some cheering. "We are just housemates so you can stop any rumours." He looked at Ted. "So on the 28th December, which is a Saturday, Jenny and I will be having a belated Christmas and New Year party and you are all invited. That includes wives and girlfriends. Neil and Alex will be coming and staying over and there will be several spare beds if you are too tipsy to travel home. Food and alcohol will be supplied but you can also bring your own if you wish."

Reg said "I will be alone."

53

Aftermath

It was Friday 31st January 1964. Renton had arrived at his desk at his usual time of 8.30 and saw that he had several crime files to attend to. Frank had checked them over so Renton knew they would be in order. He had a quick look through then his telephone rang. He answered it instinctively looking at his wristwatch, it was 09.20.

"Margery here. Ralph could you come and see the Chief now before prayers?"

"Certainly. On my way". When Margery said the word "now," that was to tell him it was serious.

Renton went up the stairs and saw Margery who waved him threw pulling her "Watch out" face.

He knocked and went in. The Chief was pacing up and down with some paper in his hand.

"Aha. Ralph, please sit down while I fume." He paced up and down and then sat down. "I had a telephone call from the Attorney General yesterday to tell me that the bounder Morton has been released into the custody of some bloody secret service. I cannot tell you how I feel. I am bloody fuming. This came, read it."

He handed Renton a letter. It was from the Attorney General's office with an endorsement from the Foreign Office.

Dear Chief Superintendent Dawson,

This letter is to tell you that an application has been made to these offices for Michael Morton to be released under the parole system so that he can continue the work that he does so superbly in South America with certain other secret services in bringing to justice and detaining those Nazis and other war criminals to be tried and punished.

Yours sincerely

The Attorney General

The Chief said "As you can see this letter is dated 27th January and it is not even signed. It undoubtedly went to the Attorney general who posted it to me. I telephoned him I was not pleasant I can say. He told me that when I read this letter Morton will already be out there with guess who? The real bloody Robert Bond! It is disgraceful. He told me that if Morton does set foot back here he will be rearrested and then go to court and then prison. Are they living in Fairyland? He is never coming back here for God's sake."

Renton said "Who put pressure on the Attorney General?"

"I rang Sir Mortimer at his home and he said it was some high-ranking case officer in MI6 who got on to the Prime Minister who in turn turned the thumbscrews and said that they probably deserved it, Miller and the others. What is the world coming to? Anyway, sorry to rant and rave I will let you get back to your desk."

Renton returned to CID and told Frank what had happened.

Several weeks later a postcard arrived addressed to Inspector Renton. It was a picture of a beach and sea. Renton turned it over it said "Hello Ralph. Greetings from Rio, no hard feelings old chap." It was signed "The one that got away."

Renton showed Frank and Reg.

Frank said "Mark my words. That cocky bastard will come back and when he does, we will put him away for good."

THE END

Printed in Great Britain
by Amazon

23977219R00109